Dopeman: Memoirs of a Snitch

Part 3 of Dopeman's Trilogy

Dopeman:
Memoirs of a Snitch

Part 3 of Dopeman's Trilogy

Dopeman: Memoirs of a Snitch

Part 3 of Dopeman's Trilogy

JaQuavis Coleman

URBAN BOOKS

www.urbanbooks.net

Urban Books, LLC
78 East Industry Court
Deer Park, NY 11729

Dopeman: Memoirs of a Snitch Copyright © 2012
JaQuavis Coleman

ISBN 13: 978-1-60162-288-4
ISBN 10: 1-60162-288-0

First Printing May 2012
Printed in the United States of America

10 9 8 7 6 5 4 3

Distributed by Kensington Publishing Corp.
Submit Wholesale Orders to:
Kensington Publishing Corp.
C/O Penguin Group (USA) Inc.
Attention: Order Processing
405 Murray Hill Parkway
East Rutherford, NJ 07073-2316
Phone: 1-800-526-0275
Fax: 1-800-227-9604

Dopeman:
Memoirs of a Snitch

Part 3 of Dopeman's Trilogy

JaQuavis Coleman

Dedication

This book is dedicated to my wife and son. I love you two forever and a day and I will always be there. I love you two from the core of my soul and would die for you without hesitation. Coleman equals Dynasty. Let us write on the walls of history.

Rest in Peace MG. Rest in peace Jake.

To my Jersey plug. . . . I would never mention ya name

Love

Prologue

Breathe in
Breathe out
Breathe in
Breathe out
The journalist sweated profusely under the black pillowcase that covered his entire head. Not hyperventilating was the only thing running through his mind as he saw nothing but complete darkness. He had been wearing the material over his head for hours and had grown anxious and the nervousness began to set in. Although he was uncomfortable, it was well worth what he was to get in return. He had the chance to interview one of the most infamous people in the modern day history. Well, the biggest in the American gangster history.

The roar of the helicopter's engine drowned out all sound and the only thing he seemed to hear was the sound of his own breathing. His heart was pounding from anxiety and it felt as if his heart was about to jump out of his chest. Two federal agents sat on either side of him as they looked down on the simple country of Canada; Toronto to be exact. They hovered thousands of feet above ground and were approaching their destination. The pilot gave the two agents thumbs up, signaling that they could finally take the pillow case off of the journalist.

Chris Nicks felt the fabric being pulled off of his face and it nearly made his bifocal glasses fall off the bridge of his nose. He quickly repositioned them on his face and looked out of the window, wondering where in the world he was. He pulled the inhaler from his inside coat pocket and immediately put it to his mouth. He inhaled the medicine and his breathing immediately returned to its normal pace. Chris smiled and looked down at the scenery. Never would he think that they were in the country of Canada. A small smile formed on his nerdy face as he thought about what was to come. He had the opportunity to interview the most legendary snitch of all time. Chris had the pillowcase over his face for hours, but it was all part of the procedure when dealing with a person who was in a witness protection program. He was ready to see the man behind the myth, who went by the name of Ball aka Braylon Kennedy. Chris Nicks took a deep breath and stared out of the window, preparing for landing on top of an unidentified building.

Ball slowly paced his lush studio apartment. The sounds of his gators clicked the floor as he rested his hands in the pockets of his finely threaded Armani slacks. A dress style he adopted from his former mentor who he eventually took the witness stand against. Ball had a neatly trimmed goatee which was speckled with shades of gray that prematurely showed up on his 34 year old face. Maybe the fear of one of the goon's of the man that he once took the stand against, coming after him made the gray hairs appear. Even ten years later, the worry of retaliation invaded his thoughts numerous times throughout a day. Ball had been anticipating the present day for two months. Every since the magazine article came out about him, he wanted to give his side of the story. Ball grabbed the glass of cognac off the table and took a small sip. He then looked down at the magazine that had a picture of his former friend walking out of a courtroom in a Armani suit with reporters surrounding him. Then it was a small picture of him in the corner with the word Snitch under it. He picked up the magazine and shook his head in frustration. He never liked snitches and was raised to believe, that if you ratted on your man, then you were not a real man yourself. It pained him to have the label put on his family's name.

Braylon "Ball" Kennedy sat down at his cherry oak table with a burning cigar inside of the ashtray in front of him. He then scanned the front page of the magazine. The headline read. . . "Inside: The Untold Memoirs of a Snitch". The sight alone made Ball sick to his stomach as he clenched his teeth tightly and knew that the article only told half the story. The doorbell chimed and Ball knew that his guest had finally arrived. He looked at his eight screen monitor and saw the journalist standing at his door. Ball grinned as he saw the skinny, nerdy guy waiting while looking up in the monitor. Ball pressed the intercom and spoke into it.

"State ya' name," Ball said as he leaned into the microphone.

"Chris Nicks . . . from FED magazine," Nicks said as he wiped his nose with the napkin in his hand. Ball suspiciously checked all of his other cameras and his paranoia sat in. It was against the rules to ever reveal one's self while under witness protection, but Ball wanted to set the record straight. He made arrangements for the journalist to come have a six hour sit-down with him, so that he could tell his side of what went down. After a few seconds of scanning his camera, he finally hit the button to buzz the journalist in. Moments later, a knock sounded and Ball approached the door. He glanced at the sawed off shotgun that sat by the door. He also clicked his handgun off safety, not taking anything lightly. He had a lot of enemies and didn't underestimate anyone. He slowly unlocked the row of deadbolts that lined his door. Ball slowly opened the door and the journalist was on the other side fixing his thick bi-focal glasses properly onto his face.

" Hell . . . hello Mr. Kennedy," Nicks said with fear evident in his voice. The trembling of his voice indicated that Nicks felt the power of Ball's boss-like swagger. Nicks extended his hand and it was noticeably shaky. Ball looked at the young man that stood in front of him and noticed that he was much younger than what he expected. He didn't look a day over twenty. *This is the kid that wrote that fucked up article about me?* He thought to himself as he looked into Nicks' eyes and saw that he had fear in his heart as he stood before him.

"Relax li'l nigga. And call me Ball . . . step in," he said in his baritone voice as he stepped to the side giving him a pathway to enter the house. Nicks stepped in and Ball immediately closed the door and locked the deadbolts back behind him; all seven of them.

"What you got in the bag?" Ball asked as he slightly raised his head noticing that the reporter had a knapsack.

"Oh, this? Just my tape recorder, notebook and my laptop," Nicks said as he handed the bag over to Ball. Ball grabbed the bag and looked through it and just as Nicks said, there were only his approved items inside. After a couple of seconds of silence, Ball returned the bag to Nicks and headed into the den not wanting to waste any time. Nicks followed Ball and looked at the gigantic house in amazement. He was in awe of the high cathedral ceilings and immaculate brown and cream colored marble floors. Although Ball was hiding out, by no means was he living like an average Joe. The closer they got to the den, the more clearly Nicks could hear the sounds of smooth jazz lightly pumping out of the speakers.

"We don't have a lot of time, so let's get to it," Ball said directly and in a 'no bull-shit' manner. "Have a seat," Ball suggested as he opened his hand toward his couch section. The large, brown leather couches looked as if they were brand new and never been sat on. The smell of the leather invaded Nicks' nostrils as he walked over to the sitting area and took a seat.

In the meantime, Ball walked over to his china cabinet and grabbed a small glass and poured himself a swallow of cognac. "Would you like a drink?" Ball asked as he cut the top and bottom of his cigar.

"No thanks, I don't drink," Nicks said as he began to pull out the equipment he needed to properly conduct the interview.

"Well, I don't see any point in wasting any more time," Ball said as he took a seat across from the reporter, placing his glass down and sitting the cigar into the ashtray. "I read your fifteen page article about what went down with me and Seven. I'm not going to lie . . . it pissed me off," Ball said as he sat back while picking up the cigar, clenching his jaws so tightly that veins formed in his neck. The tension in the room was evident and Nicks grew uncomfortable as he noticed the menacing scowl on Ball's face. Obviously, Ball had taken offense to the half-told story that made him out to be the most disloyal underboss of all time. Their story was well documented and had been seen on BET, and in many magazines over the years. But Nicks' article was so in-depth and so one-sided . . . Ball had to set the record straight.

"I know what I did was wrong and I have to live with that every single day of my life. But I had no other choice. It wasn't like I sought out Seven to take him down," Ball said as he dropped his head and thought about the man that he had betrayed and loved so much. "I had to do it," Ball whispered as he took in a deep breath and shook his head from side to side, the regret tormenting him.

"Well, that's why I'm here. Let me hear your side of the story," Nicks said as he clicked on his recorder causing the red light to switch on. He then pulled the top off of his pen and waited for Ball to proceed. Nicks was staring so intensely at the man that sat across from him. He wanted to capture every emotion, every gesture, and actually feel the pain of the man the streets called the worst snitch of all-time. He wanted to get the real story of the man that took down the biggest drug lord the Midwest had ever seen.

"Seven was one of the realest niggas I ever met. He was cut from a different cloth, ya know?" Ball said as he puffed the cigar, a habit that Seven had given him while they ran together. Seven loved cigars and cognac and before long . . . so did Ball. It was a habit he never shook. Ball smiled thinking about the times they balled out, and then a wave of sadness overcame him as he thought back. "I remember the day that I saw the police handcuff him. . . ."

Chapter One

Boss of Bosses

The eighteen-foot speedboat zoomed across the top of the ocean's water, hitting each wave at almost eighty miles per hour. Seven smiled while a cigar hung out the left side of his mouth and the sun beamed down on his skin. He looked over and saw the other speedboat was neck to neck with him while his right hand man steered the watercraft. Ordinary boatmen wouldn't dare push an $80,000 luxury watercraft to the max; but they weren't ordinary boaters. . . . they were street millionaires who just so happen to be in boats.

Seven was the head of the operation and boss of all bosses. You couldn't mention heroin in Ohio, if Seven's name wasn't somewhere in the sentence. An all-white linen shirt hung on Seven's shoulders perfectly, and he left the buttons unfastened to allow the wind to blow through the expensive fabric while displaying his slight gut. He glanced over at Ball, who was driving the other boat, and laughed aloud as he knew that he had won the race. Seven slowed down after he passed the marker and threw both of his hands up in victory. As the other boat approached, Seven looked at Ball and smiled.

"I want my money all in ones," Seven teased as they had just bet $20,000 on the thirty-second race.

"It's nothing," Ball spat back with a smile as he tossed his anchor over board and put the engine an idle. Seven did the same and put out his cigar as he looked down at his watch and saw they were right on time.

"Packages should be here any minute now," Seven whispered under his breath as he scanned over the massive ocean while he put his hand over his brow, blocking the beaming sun rays. Just as expected, a single engine jet came across the skies, leaving a trail of white smoke as the aircraft zoomed through the clouds. Ball looked in the sky and watched as duct taped packages fell from the jet and landed in the water only a few yards away from them. Seven immediately grew a grin on his face and began to think about the money he would get when he turned the powder substance that was in the packages into green bills. Seven looked over at Ball and nodded his head while giving him a smile as if he was saying "Time to get to the money," and Ball returned the smile as he rubbed his hands together.

"Yo, remember this spot . . . the drop-off is always made on the fifteenth marker," Seven instructed Ball as he pointed to the ocean marker. Ball made a mental note so he would remember where to pick up the dope next time around. Seven signaled Ball to hop over in his boat and Ball quickly did just that. Seven, while the boat was idle, guided it to the spot where the packages were dropped.

"Help me out," Seven said as he grabbed a long steel pole with a net on the end of it and began retrieving the dope from the water. Ball helped him load the oversized duffle bags onto the boat, both of them containing fifty kilos each. They both loaded it onto the boat and a patrol boat was approaching them fast.

"Ah shit . . . we got company," Ball said as he grew uneasy. He noticed a boat approaching them, which contained three uniformed men. A huge U.S. Coast Guard logo resided on the side of their speedboat and the sight alone made Ball's heart skip a beat.

"Relax. Just be calm," Seven instructed as he continued to load the bags onto the boat. "Good evening gentlemen," Seven said as shook his hands dry and rolled up his sleeves. Ball's heart began to beat rapidly as he looked at the badges on the guards that occupied the boat.

"What's going on here?" the man who seemed to be in charge asked.

"Not much. My friend and I are just enjoying the beautiful ocean," Seven said with a smirk on his face.

"Oh I see," the guard responded.

Seven reached into his glove compartment, pulled out a brown paper bag, and tossed it over to the boat where the guards were.

"Same as always," Seven said as looked into the eyes of the guard. "And smile . . . y'all making my man nervous over here," he added. Everyone, except Ball, burst into laughter as they saw the beads of sweat forming on Ball's forehead. Ball broke down and released a smile too, sensing that everything was all good.

The guard slipped the bag into his inner vest and pulled off just as quickly as he pulled up.

"It's like that, huh?" Ball asked as he couldn't believe that Seven had the police on his payroll. Seven slowly nodded his head in agreement as he pulled his cigar from his top pocket and lit it, blessing the clear air with Cuban cigar smoke.

"You trust that he won't turn on you?" Ball asked trying to understand the angles of the game.

"It's not that I trust him . . . I trust greed. I trust that the money that I'm giving him every month keeps him loyal to me. Always trust greed. . . . It will never let you down," Seven explained as he began to pull the anchor out of the water. Ball soaked up the game Seven was giving him, and he admired the way Seven looked at the game as if it was chess . . . Every move was strategic and well thought out.

"This is my last flip and I'm done with the game for good," Seven said as he sat in the driver's chair. He took a deep breath and stared into the ocean, obviously in deep thought. Seven grew a somber look on his face as new thoughts emerged in his mind. "I have to do it for Li'l Rah," Seven said referring to his seven year old son.

"How is he holding up?" Ball asked, knowing that he was suffering from leukemia.

"Not so good . . ." Seven said just before he paused and a great wave of sadness overcame him. He felt his knees began to shake almost to the point they were about to buckle. "The doctor said he has about a year left to live," Seven continued as he turned his head away from Ball, not wanting him to see the hurt in his eyes.

"Damn," Ball said under his breath as his heart dropped from of the horrible news.

"That's why I'm about to flip this last shipment and hang it up for good. I'm leaving everything to you. I'm done with this game," Seven said as he looked into the eyes of his protégé. Seven had a lot of love for Ball and in many ways he reminded him of himself. "I'm going to move to Florida with my son and make his last year the best year of his life. We'll go to Disney World every day, and we'll live life to the fullest. We are going to fight this battle head on and hope for the best."

"That sounds like a plan," Ball said not believing his ears. *He's about to give his whole empire to me?* Ball thought as he looked at Seven.

"It's all yours," Seven said as if he could hear Ball's thoughts.

"Listen man, just go . . . Leave this game alone now. Leave these bags with me and go the other way. You and Li'l Rah should just go to Florida today."

"What?" Seven asked, not understanding Ball's logic.

"You have enough to live so why take a risk and try to make extra money." Ball asked really wanting for Seven to leave for Florida at that moment. Ball had a bad gut feeling and just wanted Seven to go far away and never look back. Ball felt that the dope game would be better in his hands rather than in Seven's.

"One last time," Seven said with confidence. Seven's eyes were piercing and he was determined to follow through with his plans. He had already had his mind made up.

Ball started to contest Seven, but he decided to hold his tongue. He understood that once a man had made up his mind, it would be hard to convince him to do otherwise. Ball jumped back over to his boat and started up his engine. Seven did the same, but just before he pulled off so they could head back to shore and flood the streets with raw heroin . . . He looked over at Ball.

"Yo!" Seven yelled over.

"I love you fam," Seven said meaning every word. Ball paused and let the words sink in. He had never heard another man tell him that they loved him before. He looked into Seven's eyes and knew that the words were sincere and genuine. Seven was a real nigga and he wanted to let his protégé know that he had love for him.

"Love you too, big homie," Ball replied. Seven slowly nodded his head and quickly pushed the throttle making his boat's front end rise up.

"Double or nothing!" he yelled just before he sped away. Ball burst into laughter and quickly kicked his boat in gear, ready to race.

Minutes later they were docking their boats and ready to unload the bags into Seven's Range Rover which waited at the other side of the pier. Seven had a duffle bag over his shoulder and so did Ball. As they reached the end of the pier, Seven felt strange and stopped in his tracks. He then noticed a helicopter fly over his head and he stared at it. It seemed like everything was unfolding in slow motion. Federal agents came from every way with their guns drawn. Some were even hopping out of the water with automatic assault rifles.

"Freeze, put your motherfucking hands up," one yelled as they quickly approached. Seven smiled as he dropped the bag and put his hands up.

"Don't say anything Ball! I will have us out in the morning," Seven yelled with a small grin on his face. Ball dropped his bag and put up his hands as the feds rushed them. Ball dropped his head and knew that they would not be getting out in the morning; at least Seven wouldn't be. Ball couldn't even look Seven in the eyes . . . the game was now over.

Chapter Two

Killing Her Softly

18 months before

Braylon looked down at his watch and noticed it was just a few ticks before midnight. He took a deep breath and rested his head on the elevator's wall, waiting for it to reach his floor. Once he heard the bell chime, signaling his stop, he picked up the duffle bag that sat at his feet and headed out. He smiled as he felt the weight of the bag, knowing that it was full of dirty money, $44,000 to be exact. After her repaid his Dominican coke connect, Ralphie, he would have profited ten stacks which wasn't bad for one night's work. He had just sold two bricks of raw cocaine to a Spanish kid in Harlem who was moving heavy weight. Braylon was twenty four years old with the street knowledge of a seasoned veteran.

Braylon was dark as night, but had smooth skin and perfect white teeth that enhanced his appearance. His scraggly beard was perfectly lined, which gave him a gritty look. As the bottom of his timberlands thumped against the marble floors in his condo's hallway, he thought about how he'd almost reached his goal of stacking enough drug money so that he could relocate to California with his long-time girlfriend Zoey. Braylon approached his door and quickly scanned down the hallway making sure no one was following him. He had a bad habit of sometimes being overcautious. He placed his key into his door and stepped into his dark apartment anticipating laying his head on his pillow and getting some rest. He sat the bag full of money in his closet, tossed his car keys on the counter, and made his way to the back room while removing his leather Pelle Pelle coat along the way. Braylon reached his bedroom and was so worn-out, he didn't realize that his light had already been turned on, not like he originally left it. Just as Braylon was about to remove his gun from his waist, he saw someone burst from out of his closet. He reached for the gun, but quickly paused when he saw the intruders face . . . it was Zoey.

"Zoey!" Braylon yelled as he put his hand on his chest and took a deep breath. Zoey smiled and looked at him with her beautiful green eyes. Her slim, smooth body was on full display as she wore nothing but a small t-shirt and red stilettos.

"Don't be frightened baby. I just wanted to surprise you," Zoey said as she sexily walked over to Braylon and rested her hands on his chest while looking up at him with her big green eyes. She was very fair skinned and at times people mistook her for a white woman. She also had long jet black hair, resembling a high end fashion model. She had the petite body of a dancer but her curves were plump in all the right places.

Braylon wanted to be upset, but when he saw her green eyes he instantly calmed down and grinned. "You got me good that time, but you can't be doing that, ma. I could have popped you," he said as he grabbed her by the butt cheeks and gently lifted her off of her feet. She spread her legs and swiftly wrapped them around his waist as they began to kiss, playing with each other's tongue slowly.

"You were going to shoot me?" Zoey asked in an innocent voice as she playfully poked out her lip, giving him her baby face.

"Nah, you know better. You just caught me off guard," Braylon said as she gently squeezed her buttocks. Braylon immediately felt his manhood begin to rise in his jeans and the tingle in his tip. Braylon placed her on the vanity and stared into her eyes admiring her beauty. He always wondered what a good girl like Zoey saw in a gritty hustler like himself. They were the complete opposite, but nevertheless they were deep in love with each other. Braylon loved Zoey with all his heart and he especially loved making love to her. She was his reason for breathing and he had promised her that relocating to California to pursue her acting career was in their near future. She was the sole reason that he was taking penitentiary chances by hustling in the streets. Best friends when they were pre-teens, it eventually blossomed into a deep relationship.

"I love you Zo," Braylon whispered as he slid his hand down to Zoey's love-box. He moved her panties to the side, already knowing what she wanted. Braylon noticed that she was soaked and her moaning only turned him on more. He gently slipped two fingers inside of her while rubbing on her clitoris with his thumb. While moving his thumb in a circular motion he used his other hand to unbuckle his pants and boxers, exposing his rock hard tool.

"Put it in Braylon, please," Zoey begged in a childlike voice as she closed her eyes and enjoyed Braylon slowly finger popping her. Zoey was so wet that she began to leave a small puddle on the vanity dresser. Braylon scooped her up and laid her on the bed. He then slid off his polo shirt, exposing his tattooed upper body. He looked at Zoey and smiled as she slid off her panties and spread her legs, exposing her pink insides and clitoral erection. The sight alone almost made Braylon pop, but he held his composure and hovered over her. Just before he dropped his rod into her wetness he whispered he loved her. As he entered her, Zoey's back arched in pleasure and a small moan escaped her lips expressing her satisfaction. Braylon stroked hard and slow as he moved his hips in circles, trying to hit the right spot. He then begin to tongue kiss her collarbone gently. Fireworks . . . that's the only word to describe this particular love session. They both felt the love coming off each other, and it was one of the best feelings in the world to the both of them. Braylon momentarily stopped moving and looked into Zoey's eyes.

"I love you with all my heart," he whispered. Zoey smiled and a small tear formed in her eyes as she was overcome with love.

"I love you too," she whispered as closed her eyes anticipating him diving deep once again. They made love through the night, professing their love for one another over and over again.

Braylon guided his Range Rover through the darkened city streets, glancing in his rearview mirror as a precaution. He had executed this exact routine a million times before . . . It was a song and dance that he knew well. It was re-up time and deep in his gut he knew that this would be his last run. It was time to give up the game. At the age of twenty-three, he had peaked in the game and there was nowhere else to go but down. So before he could fall off, he was determined to exit at the top. *Just one more flip,* he thought. The vibrating BlackBerry on his passenger seat caught his attention and he smiled when he noticed Zoey's face appear on his screen. She was his world. Everything that he did was for her and he knew that he owed her everything . . . that she deserved everything, including a man that she could be proud of. Zoey was a good girl and the last thing Braylon wanted to do was risk her safety. All he wanted to do was take care of his lady and after he moved this last shipment he would have enough money saved for them to move south. The beginning of the rest of their lives was within arm's reach. He could see the finish line, now all he had to do was get to it.

He sent Zoey to voice mail to avoid the distraction that her beautiful voice would surely cause. He needed to be focused and to stay on point. He never mixed Zoey in his street affairs. Keeping her away from his business ensured her well being. His most priceless possession, he made sure that she was untouchable; unscathed by his gritty hood life. Zoey was too good for a hood nigga like Braylon and he knew it, but she stuck with him through it all. She had weathered the storm on his way to the top and now he was about to reward her with the fruits of his hard labor.

As he pulled into the lot of the abandoned ware-house, he hit his horn quickly to announce his arrival. Seconds later a Dominican kid stuck his head out of the door, confirming Braylon's presence. He motioned for Braylon to drive inside as he lifted the garage door. Braylon felt the steel nine milli that rested against his waistline, and then nodded his head as he pulled in-side. He reached over and grabbed the black duffel bag that sat beside him before stepping out of the truck. Underneath the yellow ceiling light sat Ralphie, Ball's connect, with a cigar dangling from his mouth. The smoke danced into the sky as Ralphie eyed the cards in his hand and upped his ante.

"Braylon, sit down and come play a hand," Ralphie said, never lifting his eyes from the table. Braylon looked at the other men in the room. Two Dominican men sat at the table with Ralphie while the young guy who had let Braylon in stood off in a corner, watching . . .

An uneasy feeling passed over Braylon. In all the years that he had been doing business with Ralphie, not once had he ever had casual conversation with the man. Ralphie was always short and about his paper. Their relationship had been non-existent. Their interactions were nothing more than a transaction of goods and now all of a sudden Ralphie was acting uncharacteristically. They had always done business privately and the presence of Ralphie's goons struck a sour chord in Braylon. *Just get the shit and get out,* Braylon thought as he stood with his hand beneath his jacket, palming his pistol. He kept his cool, not revealing his displeasure. On the outside he was a stone wall, but on the inside his sixth sense was urging him that something was wrong.

"Nah, I'm in and out like every other time," Braylon replied as he peered unflinchingly at Ralphie and his henchmen. "You got the stuff?"

Ralphie looked up for the first time. He could hear the apprehension in Braylon's voice. "What's got your fucking panties in a bunch? Eh?" Ralphie asked rhetorically. "Sit down for a second..."

"Nah, I'm good," Braylon said, this time more firmly.

Ralphie chuckled and then played his hand, purposefully making Braylon wait.

Braylon's patience wore thin as he watched the fat, Dominican man ignore him. He tossed the duffel bag on top of the table, interrupting their card game.

"Can we handle business?" Braylon spat.

Anger flashed briefly across Ralphie's face, but he quickly regained his composure and peeked inside the duffel bag. When he saw the different denominations of bills cluttered inside he had to contain his smile. Braylon had been a good customer of his and tonight was no different. The $60,000 in the duffel bag was enough for Braylon to cop three bricks of raw heroine.

"I've got to count it."

"It's all there but be my guest," Braylon answered.

Ralphie nodded to the henchman that sat to his right, and the man immediately stood and disappeared to the back of the warehouse along with Braylon's money. The uncomfortable silence that filled the room was so great that the sound of a leaky pipe echoed throughout the building. Braylon's senses were intensified by his intuition. He could feel the larceny in the air and in his gut he knew that Ralphie had bad intentions. The hairs on the back of his neck stood up as he stared down the young kid in the corner. He noted the bulge sticking from underneath the kid's shirt and knew that it was the butt of a gun. From experience he knew that Ralphie kept two pistols on him and he was sure that the other two goons were armed as well. He was outnumbered . . . he knew it and from the look in Ralphie's eyes, so did he.

"Yo, how long it take to count the paper? I've got somewhere to be," Braylon said.

"You rushing home to that pretty little girlfriend of yours?" Ralphie remarked as he sat back and puffed away at his Cuban cigar. "I don't blame you Braylon. If I had a hot piece like that waiting at home for me, I would be in a rush too. Is it true what they say about dancers? She must be extremely flexible."

Braylon's temperature quickly rose. "What?" he asked aggressively. Braylon knew that he had never mentioned Zoey to Ralphie, and he had for damn sure never said anything about her being a dancer. Braylon had been in the game long enough to know that there was an underlying threat behind Ralphie's friendly disposition.

"How you know about my girl? Fuck she got to do with this business?"

Ralphie stared Braylon directly in the eyes. "Calm down Braylon . . . it's my job to know about the people I deal with; nothing more, nothing less. You're good money with me Braylon. Relax."

Braylon exhaled loudly. His nerves had him on edge. There was something fishy in the air, but before his mind could figure it out Ralphie's henchman emerged from the back. "It's all there," the man announced as he passed the bag filled money back to Ralphie.

"Of course it is," Ralphie replied. Ralphie pulled a large paper grocery bag from underneath the card table and tossed it toward Braylon. It landed at his feet and Braylon bent down to peer inside. Three bricks lay neatly inside. He picked it up and as he stood, the back of his head was met with the barrel of a gun.

Click.

He heard the round as it was chambered and he instantly knew that he had messed up. "Fuck," he whispered to himself as he swallowed the lump in his throat. "It's like that? This is how you do business? After I spend good with you . . . you gon' snake me?" Braylon had copped from Ralphie three times before, but this time Ralphie decided that he didn't want to play fair. He saw Braylon as a young, black kid who could be easily taken advantage of. Ralphie was a low-level Dominican boss with high-level connections. Although he was supplying Braylon with the best . . . the dope wasn't at Ralphie's limitless disposal and when he ran out of product he decided to rob Braylon. Despite their previous dealings, Ralphie had no loyalty and now that he was in a desperate position, Braylon became his new target. Ralphie and the other men pulled their weapons from beneath the table and pointed them at Braylon.

Ralphie stood to his feet and slowly approached Braylon. "It's not personal Braylon. I actually like you kid. See when you called me to re-up I started to tell you that it was over . . . that the well ran dry. But then I thought about the $60,000 I would be missing out on. I don't miss money," Ralphie stated as he bent down and retrieved his last three bricks. "I'm keeping the dope and taking your money."

Braylon ice grilled Ralphie and the hatred he felt could be sensed throughout the room. He wanted to reach for the gun that was concealed on his waistline and pop off, but he knew logically that he had no wins. Zoey crossed his mind and he shook his head in disgrace. He needed the money that Ralphie was sticking him for and he definitely needed the dope. He had promised Zoey a better life and now he feared he wouldn't be able to deliver. With the gun pressed firmly to the back of his head he lifted his hands. He wouldn't let his pride send him to an early grave. He made a mental note that he would see Ralphie later as he opened his mouth to speak.

"You can have it. I just want to walk out of here with my life," Braylon said.

"Just like that? You think I'ma let you walk out of here and give you the opportunity to come back for me later?" Ralphie laughed in response.

"I'm not on no shit like that. All I want is to go home. I have somebody there waiting on me. You can have that sixty and the extra thirty stacks I got in the trunk," Braylon said, honestly. He was trying to show good faith. He would let Ralphie rob him for all he had as long as he left out of the place breathing.

"You think I'm stupid or something?" Ralphie asked as he relieved Braylon of his pistol. "You probably have another gun in your truck."

Braylon shook his head, "Nah, no pistol. You can have it all. Just send me out of here breathing."

Ralphie's greed overrode intellect as he looked back at Braylon's truck. "Go check it out," he told the goon who sat beside him. Braylon's labored breathing revealed the anxiety he felt as the goon went to the back of the SUV and attempted to open the trunk.

"Ralphie, it won't open!" the goon shouted as he pulled at the latch on the back of the truck.

Ralphie stuck his gun in Braylon's rib cage. "You're playing games with me Braylon?" he asked tauntingly.

Braylon winced as the tip of the gun bruised his ribs and replied, "There's a button on the inside of the truck. It releases the hatch."

"Hit the button on the inside!" Ralphie instructed, his voice revealing his eagerness. The extra thirty grand had not been something he had expected, but it was a lovely addition to the pot.

After a few minutes of searching the goon yelled, "I don't see it."

"Fucking idiot," Ralphie mumbled as he impatiently pushed Braylon toward the car. "You do it."

Braylon walked cautiously to the driver side with Ralphie right behind him. With his automatic start in his pocket he secretly hit the button that turned his interior lights off. Once he was inside the truck, he leaned down and reached underneath the passenger seat. Ralphie thought he was reaching for the button to pop the trunk. He had no idea that Braylon always kept an extra burner underneath his passenger seat. The feeling of the gun in his hand gave Braylon a sense of security in the tense situation. Braylon knew that it was a great possibility that it may have been his day to die, but he was gonna make sure that somebody went with him. If Zoey had to grieve him, he was going to make another bitch across town a widow right along with her.

With Ralphie standing directly behind him, Braylon sent his size eleven Timberland boot slamming into Ralphie's groin area. The wind was knocked out of Ralphie as he instantly doubled over, grabbing at his crotch. Braylon started his vehicle and put the car in reverse. Without thinking twice he hit the gas, running down the goon that was behind his car.

Boom! Boom! Boom!

Gunshots erupted throughout the building as Ralphie put Swiss cheese holes in the body of Braylon's truck.

Braylon racked his gun and stuck his hand out the window, firing back wildly at Ralphie and his henchman as he drove simultaneously. Braylon was fucking the warehouse up as he barreled his Range Rover into the card table in an attempt to murder the young kid who was using it as cover. Enraged, Braylon jumped from his truck and ran up on the injured Hispanic kid.

Boom!

The hollow tip that Braylon put into the kid's forehead silenced him forever. Braylon snatched the kilos of heroin and the black duffel bag up from the ground before hopping back into his truck. Braylon was like a marksman with his pistol as he shot it out with Ralphie and his goons, but the bullets that riddled the Range Rover were dangerously close to ending his life. *I've got to get the fuck out of here,* he thought as his heart pounded in fear and anxiety. Braylon put the truck in reverse and prepared to exit out of the garage, but a bloody Ralphie stood between his Range and the exit. Braylon watched as Ralphie raised his gun. Just as Ralphie pulled the trigger Braylon stepped on the accelerator, sending the car flying backwards. Ralphie jumped out of the way just in time as Braylon blew past him and swerved out onto the deserted city street.

Screeeech!

His tires burned the pavement below as he came to a stop before he switched gears. Before he could even put the truck in drive, he felt the bullet as it ripped through his right shoulder.

"Aghh!" he hollered as his entire right side erupted in excruciating pain. Braylon ducked down as he returned fire on Ralphie and desperately grasped his bleeding shoulder. Braylon threw the truck into the right gear and sped off into the night, leaving Ralphie firing at him in the distance as Braylon looked at him through the rearview mirror.

Braylon raced through the city streets in paranoia as he gripped his arm to try and stop the bleeding. He really needed to go to the hospital, but knew that it would draw too much attention. He had the resident hood doctor on speed dial and decided that he would call him once he arrived home. He looked over at the dope that sat in the seat next to him. He had gotten off with the money and the product, but at that moment they didn't seem to be worth all of the trouble. Ralphie had tried to kill him and although Braylon had been able to take out his goons, Ralphie was still breathing. He would undoubtedly come after him. *The next time I see that fat mu'fucka, I'm murking him . . . no questions asked,* Braylon thought as his nostrils flared and he bent three unnecessary corners just to ensure that he was not being followed. Paranoia consumed him as his blood shot eyes surveyed his surroundings and his neck sat on a constant swivel.

He couldn't believe that Ralphie had set him up. Braylon was positive that Ralphie had intended to kill him and the fact that Ralphie was aware of where he rested his head at night had Braylon shook. He pulled up to his home and sat in the driveway for fifteen minutes as he tried to detect any movement inside. Everything appeared to be the same as he had left it, but this still didn't ease the worry from his heart. He reloaded a fresh clip into his gun before grabbing the duffel bag and stepping out of the truck. The familiarity of his home allowed him to breathe easier, but he had a nagging suspicion that he just couldn't shake. There was no way he would sleep on Ralphie. Now that Ralphie had shown Braylon pure shade, Braylon wouldn't be caught slipping again.

The silence in his house caused goose bumps to form on his arm as Braylon went from room to room, turning on lights . . . letting his gun lead the way. He called Zoey's name but got no answer. For some odd reason, he felt like someone was in the house. He called for her once more, but again . . . nothing. Thoughts of Ralphie sending his goons to wait on him had him paranoid. He was ready to pop something. His nerves were shattered because he knew that he could have easily been getting tags on his toes at that very moment. Braylon finally calmed down and took a deep breath. *What a day,* he whispered as he shook his head and lowered his gun, realizing that he was tripping. He knew that Zoey was probably at the dance studio practicing late so he had time to clean himself up before she came home. He went into his room and emptied the contents of the duffel bag onto his bed. He removed his blood soaked shirt, wincing as he moved his bloody shoulder. The bullet had gone in and out so he decided that he wouldn't go to the hospital. Braylon tried to rotate his arm but a sharp pain shot threw his entire body. As he raised his head, he heard the sound of footsteps sneaking up behind him. Gun already in hand and with a hair trigger Braylon turned around and fired.

Boom!

Zoey's eyes bulged from her head as her mouth dropped in an "O" of protest as the bullet entered the center of her head and exited out of the back of her skull.

"Noo!" Braylon shouted as a crimson dot appeared on Zoey's forehead. As if time slowed down, he watched as Zoey's legs gave out from underneath her. She fell in slow motion . . . first to her knees and then face first into the carpet.

"No . . . no . . . Zoey," Braylon pleaded as he dropped the gun and felt his knees began to get weak. He then rushed to her side, pulling her up onto him for support as he collapsed onto the floor. He called her name repeatedly, begging her to live...to breathe, but it was too late. She had died on impact. Her eyes stared back lifelessly as Braylon picked her up and cradled her as her limp body dangled from his arms. Braylon let out a series of thunderous roars that came from the bottom of his gut. Tears began to form and fall as he cried like a baby, knowing that he had just mistakenly took the life of his one true love.

"I'm sorry baby. I'm so sorry. Please wake up," he whispered as he rocked her back and forth and gently kissed her forehead, hoping that she could somehow come back to life. Deep inside he knew she was gone. Her body was limp and there was no denying that her heart had stopped. He knew it because for a brief moment his heart had stopped also. The moment he had pulled the trigger his life had also ended.

Chapter Three

This Can't be Life

Braylon sat with the screw face as his eyes roamed the men around him. He didn't trust any of them and the ones who had tried to befriend him or take him under their wing aroused even more skepticism. There was nothing friendly about a nigga locked up. They almost always had hidden agendas, but Braylon wouldn't even give them room to plot on him. He was prepared to do hard time. He would body a nigga before he let anyone chump him or step on his toes. The beast in him had lay dormant for awhile. Yes, he had put in work considering his profession, but overall life with Zoey . . . or better said, the love of Zoey had tamed him. Losing her was his breaking point. No longer would he think before he acted. He was throwing caution to the wind . . . it was all about survival and it was always of the fittest. The strong would devour the weak and he refused to be the latter.

As he pondered his circumstances he had to fight with himself to let go of the past. There was no point in looking back. To remember the curves of Zoey's body or the graceful tone of her dancer's back would only incite a yearning in him. To recall her laugh or the softness of her touch against his face would only make him miss her more. The unfortunate fact was that he would never see her again. He hadn't meant to take her life,

but despite his regrets and his pleas for God's forgive-
ness, he would never get to stare into her eyes again in
this lifetime. Their moment in time had passed and he
wasn't even good for a bouquet of flowers on her grave.
He couldn't even cherish her memory because he was
caged like an animal. The entire situation overwhelmed
him, but it was out of his hands. God couldn't have con-
structed this plan. There was too much pain, too much
bad, too much sin for HIM to be involved. Hustling
had gotten him paid. He had felt the adrenaline and
prestige that came along with being up and coming on
the drug scene, but now he was living the flip side and
experiencing all the pitfalls that came with it as well.
Death, destruction, incarceration, loneliness, deceit...
all those things told the story of his life. As his cell door
opened a C.O. yelled, "Kennedy, you have a visitor!"

Braylon heard his last name as it was called out,
but he ignored it. There wasn't anyone on the outside
who would visit him. He knew Boobie didn't do the
jail thing and he respected it. Nobody wanted to hang
around speaking through plexi-glass and reminiscing
about the way things used to be. The only thing that
mattered was what was, and his reality consisted of
nothing but bars and steel.

"Kennedy!" the C.O. called with irritation lacing his
tone.

Curious, Braylon stood and peeked his head out of
his cell. The officer nodded and said, "Next time you
will forfeit the visit if I have to call your name twice."

Knowing that arguing with a county jail cop was
pointless, Braylon shook his head and pulled up his tan
Dickie pants as he sauntered into the visiting room. He
stared around the room looking for a familiar face but
found none.

"This a joke a' something man?" he asked as he looked back at the C.O. in confusion.

"Booth four," he instructed.

Braylon peered at the man sitting on the other side of the glass in booth four. *Fuck is he?* He asked himself as he walked over and sat down, reaching for the telephone receiver.

"Yo I know you fam?" he asked.

The dark skinned man didn't respond immediately, but instead took in Braylon's appearance, causing Braylon to do the same. He noted the diamonds that crowded his wrist watch, the low cut caeser, and Sean John apparel. Braylon kept his circle tight so he was positive that he had never dealt with the man before.

"Somebody sent you? You got a message for me?" he asked with hostility, thinking that the guy was one of Ralphie's goons.

"Calm down Braylon. I'm here to help you," the man said.

"Fuck out of here with that shit duke. I don't even know you," Braylon shot back. "I know you got two seconds to start talking before I get up and walk up out of here though. What you here for?"

The man leaned into the glass to avoid anyone else overhearing what he was about to say.

"My name is Dame Reed . . . and I'm an undercover federal agent for the Drug Enforcement Agency," he stated.

"Conversation's over," Braylon said as he stood up from the table abruptly while slicing his hand across his neck, signaling that it was a wrap. He walked away before the man even had a chance to protest. *I don't have shit to talk to that mu'fucka about,* Braylon thought as he went back to his cell. He had absolutely no interest in assisting Detective Reed. If there were more real niggas in the world then he wouldn't be in the position he was in. *Pigs walking around looking like real live hood niggas,* Braylon thought. *I'd hate to be in his crosshairs. They'll never see him coming.* Braylon didn't want anything to do with Reed, but shaking the detective would prove difficult.

The next day Braylon was escorted into a private visiting room where attorneys usually met with their clients. When Dame Reed walked in Braylon stood in defiance.

"Sit down," Reed said, with authority.

"C.O.!" Braylon called while shaking his head in disgust at the Detective.

"If you ever want to see life outside of these walls again, you'll sit down and hear me out," Reed stated seriously, arousing Braylon's attention.

Braylon looked at Reed trying to read him, but he emulated a street cat so well that he didn't wear his heart on his sleeve. Reed wore a serious poker face as he nodded to the chair, signaling for Braylon to take a seat. Braylon walked to the chair and sat down reluctantly as Reed sat down in the chair across from him.

"At least you look like your own kind now," he shot as he sat with both hands nestled comfortably behind his head. The cheap black suit that the detective wore revealed his true identity and the badge that was proudly clipped to his belt confirmed it.

"Listen Kenneth," Reed said.

"Braylon," he interrupted. "The name is Braylon."

"Right, Braylon," Reed said with a smirk. "I've been following your case since the moment you were arrested and although you couldn't convince a jury that the murder of your girlfriend was a mistake . . . I believe you. I also believe that you would have never been caught up on drug charges if this incident never occurred. You're smart . . ."

"Man what do you want?" Braylon said irritably as he sat back against the back of the chair and extended one leg outward. The detective was doing too much ass kissing for Braylon's liking and was acting as if they had something in common. He didn't even want it to be said that he had dealings with a cop. He knew what it would look like, him holding secret meetings with a narc, and he didn't want to go down that road. The life of a snitch behind bars was something he didn't want to experience. He didn't need that label put on him.

"I'm here to give you your freedom back," Reed stated, unflinchingly.

For the first time Braylon looked the Detective in the eye. He had his attention, but Braylon knew that his freedom wouldn't be granted for nothing. It would come at a high cost.

"Oh, yeah? How you plan to do that?" he asked sarcastically.

Dame Reed rubbed his neatly trimmed goatee and leaned into the table as his hands folded on top of it. "I'm serious Braylon. There's a program that you would be perfect for. We've established a drug cooperation task force that reduces, and in your case pardons, first time convicted felons. We don't want you Braylon. We want to catch the men you used to cop from . . . we are hunting the highest level dealers and suppliers," Reed said as he stared at Braylon intently. "All you have to do is get in with the right people, make a few moves in the street. We will supply you with everything you need to play the part."

"I ain't a fucking snitch," Braylon replied.

"I didn't call you one," Dame answered. "But you don't strike me as a stupid man. My organization and I have chosen you out of thousands of inmates who would surely jump if given this same opportunity."

"I'm not a puppet. I don't scratch my head if it don't itch and I don't jump at every opportunity I'm offered. Like I said, you can go find one of them other hoe ass niggas in here cuz I ain't no rat," Braylon seethed angrily. Braylon stood tall and didn't break. In his eyes this little rendezvous was over.

"So you're just going to give up your freedom that easily? You're going to rot in here for the rest of your life instead of making something good out of a bad situation. What about Zoey? Did she die in vain?" Dame asked.

"Don't speak about her," Braylon said. His voice was so low when he spoke that it sounded like a whisper, but it carried the weight of a threat all the same.

"She wouldn't want you to die inside these walls. Don't you want to be able to at least visit her at her gravesite or put flowers on her head stone?" Dame asked. The sorrow that passed over Braylon's expression let Dame know that he had finally hit a nerve. *Bingo,* the narcotics detective thought. He had found the angle that would sway Braylon into seeing things his way. "All the wrong that you contributed to the streets . . . give some good back to it. It's not about being a snitch. Be a man and stand accountable for the things that you've done. Do it for Zoey . . . she was a good girl. She was going places and now she's going nowhere. Think about all the other Zoey's out there . . . all the other young innocent ladies who fall victim to the flip side of the game."

"Why me? Why you barking up my tree with all this?" Braylon asked as his inner guilt began to seep out, tainting his judgment. He was plagued with visions of Zoey and he closed his eyes to stop himself from feeling too much. Braylon stood but the idea of being trapped in his tiny cell, alone with his thoughts, was more challenging than facing Dame. His wounded heart bled fresh emotion as he paced back and forth in turmoil.

"Fuck!" he exclaimed as he put both hands on the table and put his head down in disgrace.

There was no way that he could block out all that he was feeling. He was going through too much inside and the anger on top of resentment boiled to the surface. He had told Zoey he was sorry a thousand times in his mind. He hadn't even been able to attend her funeral services because he had no legal ties to her. She wasn't his wife and the system didn't recognize or even acknowledge their connection. So he was forced to mourn her from his cage and miss seeing her face one last time. At that moment he felt like he had nothing to lose. He needed to go to her grave . . . to see her name spelled out on the marble stone. He wanted nothing more than to have the ability to go to her and speak to her even though he would never hear her speak back. All of those things are what made him ache to be free.

"Why me?" he asked again, this time as a few tears snuck out of his eyes. He quickly brushed them away before looking at Dame.

"Because you've lived it . . . you walk like them, talk like them . . . you are them Braylon, and we need someone like you who can get inside and not arouse suspicion. At the end of this thing, your testimony will put the right people behind bars. You don't deserve the hand you've been dealt, but it's all you got. Now you have to play your cards right. Whether we get a conviction or not . . . at the end of this thing you get to walk away; free. Just for your participation you walk away from all of this with an expunged record," Reed said.

With Zoey on his mind and nothing to lose he said, "Okay. I'll do it. I want out of here as soon as possible."

His ears received the words as if he wasn't the one who had spoken them and he could not believe what he had been reduced to. A bottom feeder . . . a cold hearted rat. He was about to become what he had once hated and he was about to commit to do the one thing he swore he never would. Snitch.

Chapter Four

First Lady of the Streets

Braylon looked around the grungy motel room and shook his head in disbelief. He only had a small plastic bag to his name which was the only thing he could call his own. Inside the bag were his wallet, toothbrush, and small picture of him and Zoey. He looked down at the bag and took out the picture. Zoey smiled so bright while draped in his arms. It was a picture of them at a park, a picture that Braylon had a stranger take for them. The picture used to bring him joy but now it only seemed to magnify the guilt that weighed heavily on his heart. Braylon felt a tear forming in the corner of his eye and a blink propelled it down his face. He tasted the salty tear as he continued to stare at the picture of his beautiful love. He quickly wiped the tear away and kissed the picture just before propping it up on the dirty alarm clock that sat on the night stand.

Dame had dropped him off at the motel and told him that to wait there until he received further instructions. He was in a new city, a new environment, and it all seemed like a dream. Just forty eight hours ago, he was mentally preparing himself to serve a life sentence. Braylon looked at the paper with the address on it Braylon laid back in his bed and closed his eyes, preparing for his meeting in the morning.

***

Braylon looked at the address on the paper to make sure he was at the right place. He threw the government issued Mercedes Benz in park and stared at what seemed to be an abandoned building. He honestly thought about throwing the car in reverse and heading toward the nearest highway and go on the run.

"I should leave and take my chances," Braylon whispered as he shook his head in disbelief. He knew that the car he was driving probably had a tracking device on it somewhere, so the odds were against him if he bailed. "Fuck!" he yelled as he hit the steering wheel with both hands. He then took the keys out of the ignition and headed into the back entrance. The big metal door was unlocked as he pulled it open and it seemed as if it weighed a thousand pounds. When Braylon entered he noticed it was a dimly lit boxing gym. The smell of old leather and moisture filled the air as he slowly walked in, wondering where Dame was. *I think this is the place,* Braylon thought as he slowly made his way to the middle of the floor. All of a sudden, the lights slowly began to pop on and what once was a faintly lit room became a bright open space.

"Mr. Kennedy," a voice came from a distance, making Braylon turned around in a full circle trying to see where it was coming from. Dame came out of the shadows and exposed himself. He was carrying a black duffle bag. He approached Braylon and tossed the duffle bag at his feet. "That's one hundred thousand dollars in there." Dame said as he intensely stared at his new informant.

"What am I supposed to do with this?" Braylon asked as he glanced down at the bag.

"Pick the bag up and follow me. I'm about to show you." Dame said as he turned his back and headed to the back office. Braylon took a deep breath and reluctantly pick up the bag, following Dame. When Braylon entered the room, there were about five other people sitting in the office, which was set up like a small class-room. They were all sitting in front of a bulletin board as Dame stood in front of them all. Braylon stopped in his tracks and scanned everyone in there, almost embarrassed to be present in the room.

"Have a seat," Dame said as he waved his hand toward the empty chair reserved for him. Braylon slowly took a seat and a young, slim, black guy extended his hand attempting to greet Braylon.

"Psst," Braylon sucked his teeth and brushed past the man as he took his seat.

"Everybody, I want you to meet . . ." Dame said as he looked at Braylon.

"Ball . . . y'all can call me Ball." Braylon said not wanting to put his government out there like that.

"Meet Ball. He's the informant that is going to attempt to infiltrate Seven's organization. This is the team that is going to take down that son of a bitch." Dame looked over at Braylon and then proceeded to brief the crew. Dame stepped to the side revealing the bulletin board. At the top of the list was a mug shot taken of Seven a few years ago for drug possession. Just under his picture were lines that led to a couple guys and a female. It was the chain of command for Seven's entire organization. He pointed to the girl first.

"This is the beautiful Lola Banks. Don't let the good looks fool you. This bitch is connected and is as ruthless as they come. She's a one-time felon from Harlem. We don't know too much about her . . . just that she plays with the big boys and has a reputation in the streets that is strong as any man. She moves heavy weight and is considered Seven's right-hand woman. She had a couple run-ins with the law, but nothing major. The only thing we know for sure is that she is the daughter of the infamous Bunkie Green . . . one of the biggest heroin movers back in the early nineties. He ran with Lucas back in the day. We believe that she allied Seven with some of her father's old connects. Most people refer to her as the first lady of the streets."

Braylon immediately noticed the beauty of the woman that Dame described as ruthless. She seemed like she was straight out of a Vogue magazine. The surveillance photos seemed to catch her in the best light and they looked more like model snapshots rather that stakeout flicks. Braylon listened closely as Dame explained the magnitude of Seven's drug operation and empire. Braylon could tell by the look in Dame's eyes that he wanted to take Seven down badly. It almost seemed personal.

Dame continued, "We are sending Bray . . . excuse me . . . We are sending Ball in for first contact to try to establish a connection. We only have one chance to get close to Seven so we have to make this count," Dame said as he slowly paced the front of the room. "We were waiting for them to slip up and they finally did. The fight of the century is this weekend in Vegas and guess who will be there? We can finally put Seven in a spot at a certain time. One week ago Lola slipped up. She booked ten front row seats at the big fight . . . just what we were waiting for. Mind you, these seats are twenty thousand a piece. Only celebrities and wealthy men will be in this area. You have to blend in and we will equip you with everything you need to do so. We're going to seat you close to him and let you do your thing. The goal is to establish a connection with Seven," Dame said as he stopped pacing and looked directly at Braylon.

Braylon began to realize that it was getting real and he wanted to push the envelope as far as he could. He smirked and decided to see how far Dame would go.

"Well, if you want me to play the part . . . I'll have to look the part, you feel me?" he said while rubbing his hands together and looking Dame straight in the eyes. "I'll need a Rolex, a custom one. . . ."

"No problem. It's done."

Ball looked at Dame and saw that he was dead serious. So Ball decided to keep going. "Also, I'ma need a Maybach . . . the Phantom joint." He said naming his dream car. Dame paused for a second and then grabbed an envelope and handed it to Ball.

"We already rented you one for the week. You have a state issued ID, driver's license, and car keys to that Phantom in there."

Ball couldn't believe his eyes as he looked into the bag. He knew that it was time to do his job, even though he dreaded it. . . . it had to be done in return for his freedom. Next stop: Vegas.

Chapter Five
Scared Money Don't Make None

It was the night of the fight of the century. The heavy-weight champ of the world, Donte Diggs, had been favored to win the fight 3 to 1, and instead of a heavy weight championship fight, it looked more like a red carpet event. Flashing lights, exotic cars, stretch limos, and A-list celebrities, all made up what was to be a night to remember. Braylon took a deep breath as he hid behind the tinted window of a cocaine white Maybach, sitting in the back seat of course. He looked over at the thick Latino woman who was sitting next to him in a sparkly red dress. Actually, she was an undercover police officer who Dame had assigned to escort Braylon undercover. Braylon rolled his eyes and looked out of the window, still hating cops to the core of his soul. He watched people stare at the car and squint their eyes, trying to figure out who was in the luxury car that cost damn near a quarter million dollars. Braylon always wanted to ride in the backseat of a Maybach . . . but not like this. He was riding in his dream car; but he was riding as a snitch and that shamed him. "This some bullshit," Braylon whispered under his breath as he shook his head from side to side and then took the shot of Patrón that sat in his cup holder.

"Let's do it," he said as he slammed his cup down and glanced over at his date who was putting the finishing touches of her make-up on. Braylon closed his eyes and took a deep breath as he contemplated bailing out on the operation and taking his odds on the run from the law. The reality of his situation stopped him from jumping ship and Braylon decided go head and go through with an act that went against all of his beliefs. . . . snitching.

As the chauffeur opened the door, the massive sound of people and chatter overwhelmed Braylon and he slowly placed his Mauri gator shoe on the red carpet. That's when he felt the buzz the entertainers often talk about. All eyes were on him as flashes and questions were directed at Braylon as he stepped out. He buttoned the last two buttons that went to his tight-fitting, gray Armani suit. He smoothly checked his cufflinks, and then reached his hand in the car to help his date out the vehicle. It was the beginning of what was too be a long road of grand deception.

Seven puffed on his Cuban cigar as he sat in the back dressing room watching the champ shadowbox and prepare himself mentally for the fight, while his entourage stood around him giving him words of encouragement. Seven looked over at Lola and tapped his watch, signaling for her to retrieve his Russian friend who was sitting front row awaiting the fight to begin.

Lola Banks was the daughter of Ohio's legendary heroin Kingpin. . . . Bunkie Green. She followed in her father's footsteps and got into the dope game at an early age. While other teenage girls were chasing niggas and dreams, Lola was using her father's name to get her into the right circles and eventually linked up with Seven. She was a hustler to the core and was infatuated with fast money. She was dark as night, but with smooth skin and pearly white teeth. She stood five foot eight and with long legs, resembling a ghetto Naomi Campbell. She was a beautiful as they came, but just as deadly. She wore a small black dress, complimented by Louboutin red bottom heels. Her hair was tied back tightly, displaying her GS tattoo which stood for Goon Squad and identified her affiliation with Seven's crew. Lola took her time as she made it to the main floor and amongst the 50,000 people in attendance. She made her way to the front row, where only millionaires and important spectators sat. Mostly rich men and A-list celebrities filled those seats, but her crew was there front and center. She finally reached the person who Seven had sent her to get. A powerful Russian man who was one of Seven's business associates. She bent down to whisper in his ear and he immediately stood up and Lola escorted him to the back where Seven and the champ waited.

Meanwhile, Seven was in the back talking to Diggs.

"You know I got the bank on you tonight, my nigga. I need you to go hard." Seven said just after he made smoke circles from his Cuban cigar.

"I got you fam. This one is going to be easy, baby. How much?" the champ said as he slightly raised his chin and grinned, knowing that his man had a lot riding on him.

"Two mil," Seven said in a low tone being modest while returning the smirk. Just as Seven let the words escape his mouth, Lola and the tall, blonde haired Russian man entered the dressing room. Seven and the champ's attention focused on them as they walked in. Seven raised his cigar and signaled for them to come over. Seven wanted to introduce his friend to the undisputed champion of the world. The Russian walked over and Seven introduced them. "Champ this is my good friend, Mikell. Mikell, meet the champ." Seven said. Mikell spoke English but he nodded his head and grinned and the champed did the same.

Although Mikell spoke little English, he and Seven had a great business relationship. Money was a universal language and in the drug game it was all that mattered. Mikell was also a big gambler and Seven had invited him out to Vegas to meet the champ and place a seven figure bet on Diggs. The Russian was impressed that Seven knew the champ personally and that only made Mikell respect Seven even more. Gambling wasn't the only reason Mikell came to meet Seven in Vegas. Seven was solidifying a fifty kilo deal in the midst. Seven usually went through the Diamond Cartel for his dope, but he wanted to test out another source. Seven potentially would begin copping from the Russian with the raw from that day forward. So in Seven's eyes this trip was business and pleasure all rolled in one.

"I have very large money on you tonight." The Russian said in broken English as he threw a hand on the champs shoulder. "Kill him for me my friend." The Russian stated.

"I got 'em," the champ replied as he looked at the Mikell and then back at Seven. "I will check you out after the fight. Party at my house, cool?" the champ said to Seven.

"No doubt. See you later on my nigga."

"A'ight, one," the champ said just before he pounded Seven's hand and returned to the table to begin to get taped up for the fight. Seven, along with Mikell and Lola, headed down to their front row seats and get ready to view the fight. Seven glanced a couple of rows back and saw members of the Goon Squad in attendance and he nodded to one of them, letting them know to watch his back. The goon nodded back to confirm that he was on his job. It seemed as if the Goon Squad was there to enjoy the fight, but that was the furthest from the truth. They were solely there to protect their boss by any means necessary. While every other person in the building would have their eyes glued to the ring, the goon's would be watching anybody and everyone around Seven.

Ball sat in his seat and watched as the undercards fought. People were filing in just in time to see the main event. Everybody was rooting for the champ to knockout the no name opponent. Ball knew better though. He was an avid boxing fan and knew that the champ had problems with southpaw fighters. He really believed that it was the night that the champ would get knocked out. He probably was the only person in the building besides the underdog's corner that believed he would win. Ball looked around and noticed that stars and celebrities were all around him. He couldn't believe his eyes. The first couple of Hip Hop were seated a couple seats down from him and the NBA phenom, King James was a row behind him. He was definitely in foreign territory but he loved every moment of it.

The lady he was with leaned over and whispered in his ear, "There goes Lola Banks." Ball immediately looked at the woman coming down the aisle and she was far more beautiful in person. She wore a tight fitting black dress and six inch heels, red bottoms of course. Her wide hips were on full display as she swayed her assets back and forth, making her way to the front row seat. She was accompanied by a white man in a well-tailored suit. Just as they made their way to the seat a wave of young men wearing street clothes and heavy jewelry came down the aisles. None of them looked to be over twenty-one, but they all looked like money. These were the Goon Squad, which were Seven's young killers and protection. They definitely let their presence be felt as they took their seats in a row entirely reserved for them.

Ball ordered a mixed drink and just sat back and observed. His date wasn't much of company so he remained silent. Just as the main event was about to start, Ball saw the man of the hour walk down the aisle. It was Seven. He had a cigar in his mouth and a well-tailored Armani suit hung perfectly on his body. His Creed cologne invaded people's nostrils as he walked by and everyone could feel the star power enter the room as he strolled by. He stopped and slapped hands with a few celebrities before finding his seat in the front row, right next to Lola. The show was about to begin and Ball had to find his way in. Ball grew butterflies in the pit of his stomach as he watched Seven's movements. He never in a million years thought that he would be on the opposite side of the law. Everything happened so fast. He downed his drink and shook his head in guilt. The announcer began to introduce the fighters for the main event and the game had begun.

"Stop playing with this nigga!" Seven screamed as he stood up in frustration. Diggs was man-handling the underdog with ease. The crowd was on fire and everyone was on their feet cheering and rooting for a knockout. Seven was licking his chops knowing that he was about to come up on the big payday. He and all of his associates had a handsome wager on the odds of the champ winning. The bell rung just before the champ could knock the underdog out and the crowd cheered on, wanting more. Ball sat back and watched as Seven talked shit and enjoyed himself with his friends and he wondered how he would approach him. Ball had been watching the fight closely and knew that the champ had a great chance of losing if he didn't win before the fourth round. The champ had no stamina and always had trouble with left-handed boxers; the challenger was a lefty.

Seven laughed and smacked hands with Lola and bragged about the new car he would buy with his winnings from the fight. Ball was going out on a limb and acted without thinking.

"Put your money where ya' mouth is homeboy! Diggs bouta get knocked out!" Ball yelled as he looked straight at Seven. Seven frowned and turned around, looking to see who was talking reckless about his man.

"You talking to me?" Seven said as he pointed at his own chest and looked around in confusion.

"Yeah, I'm talking to you," Ball said with sinister smile. Immediately the goons stood up and all attention went on Ball. Ball looked around and saw eight pair of eyes on him and he began to feel caged in.

"What's up homie? We got problems?" One of the goons asked as they all stuck their hands in their waist and hoodies, ready to pop off in front of cameras and all. They just didn't give a fuck about human life. That's why Seven had them on his team. They were all young, wild, and thought they had a lot to prove.

Seven raised his hand, signaling for his goons to back down. He then focused his attention back to Ball. "Yo, how much you got to bet?" Seven asked.

"I got whatever," Ball yelled over the crowd's chatter as he stood up and reached into his pocket. He pulled out a big bankroll and held it up for everyone to see. "Ten racks sound good?"

"Bet! I'll take that li'l ass money from you. Easy!" Seven said as he returned the smile and slowly nodded his head.

"This fight just got a little bit more interesting," Ball said as he turned around just in time to see the fight begin once again.

The boxers emerged from their corners and went at it. The fatigue started to show in the champ and just like that. . . . Bang! He got caught with a left hook and rocked to sleep! The fight was over and the whole crowd erupted. Ball had never heard anything so loud. Flashing lights erupted and bells rung. It was a wrap. Ball had just won ten thousand dollars and also gained the attention of Seven. Seven clenched his jaws so tightly and slammed his fist against the armrest. His Russian friend buried his face in his hands because he had just lost a small fortune. He whispered in Lola's ear and stormed out. Ball smiled and reached out his hand as Seven went by. Seven dismissed his gesture and brushed right past him. Ball stood there looking dumb with his hand out as Seven exited the arena. Lola came up seconds later and handed Ball a roll of money.

"That should be enough. If there's extra, keep the change." She said as she briefly stood in front of him. Before Ball could answer, she was headed out. He had made his first contact.

Seven made his way out of the back entrance of the MGM, with Lola and the members of the Goon Squad by his side. Seven was irate that he lost the bet, but kept his poker face and showed no sign of it. He stopped just before he reached the back exit and slid off his jacket and handed it to his henchmen.

"Yo, put this on and leave out of the front." Seven said as he knew feds were potentially watching him. The henchman was about Seven's build and same skin complexion, so Seven was about to put up a smoke screen for whoever was watching so he could enjoy himself for the night.

"And you two . . . go with him," Lola ordered as she began to put on her mink so they could exit through the back in the tinted SUV that waited for them.

"Send those feds in that black van on a ride around the city for a couple of hours. That should keep them busy for a while," she instructed with a slight grin on her face. Seven and his crew were always a step ahead of the authorities so this was regular procedure for them. The henchmen followed her orders and left only Lola and Seven standing at the back entrance.

"Yo, bring me that nigga I made the bet with to me, pronto," Seven ordered as he unloosened his tie and wiggled his neck, getting more comfortable. He wanted to know how the mystery man knew that Diggs would lose. Seven understood that the man knew something that he didn't know and he was dying to find out the inside scoop. Lola nodded her head in agreement and like that . . . it was done. Seven proceed out of the back entrance and into the car that waited out back.

Ball smiled as he flipped through the crispy one hundred dollar bills. He and the undercover cop rode in the back of the Maybach and had just pulled off the lot of the MGM Grand. He completed his first assignment which was to establish contact with Seven. Now his task was to go back to Ohio and try to establish an actual connect. As they pulled back onto the road to go and meet Dame who was waiting at the airport for them, Ball saw an all-black truck pull up alongside them. Seconds later, an identical truck pulled up in from of them.

"What the fuck?" he said aloud and just as the words came from his mouth the truck in front of them stopped abruptly, making their driver come to screeching halt. Before they realized what was going on, Seven's goons jumped out of the van and immediately approached the car. They opened the doors and quickly snatched Braylon out of the car. It all happened so fast that Braylon's head was spinning. The next thing he knew, he was being stuffed into a truck and sitting next to Seven in the back seat of the truck.

"I'm Seven," he said as he puffed on a cigar and looked straight forward without flinching. He remained calm and took his time before he spoke. "Now, the question is . . . who the fuck are you? How did you know my man was going down?" Seven said wondering if Braylon had an inside scoop on Diggs throwing the fight. Because if so, Seven was going to have Diggs whacked for causing him to lose all of that money.

"I just study boxing, that's all," Braylon said nervously as he looked to the opposite side and saw the burly goon giving him the ice grill. "You see. The last time Diggs lost was when he was an amateur and it was against a lefty similar to his opponent. I also knew if it went over four rounds he would go down. I didn't have an inside tip . . . I just know boxing." Braylon carefully explained himself. Seven listened closely and liked Braylon's style. The li'l nigga knew what he was talking about and if he had met him a day before he would have cleaned up on the betting circuit.

"So where are you from?" Seven said seeing an opportunity to get a source of boxing knowledge, being that he was a heavy gambler.

"I'm from Ohio; Columbus to be exact." Ball said reciting what Dame had told him to say.

"Is that right? Those seats you were seating in cost a pretty penny. So what you do?" Seven asked.

"I'm in the distribution business," Ball responded.

"Oh yeah?" Seven answered, already guessing that that was what he was in to. A young man with money . . . it wasn't hard to figure out. Either you play ball, rap, or move weight. Seven understood that.

"I will be getting in touch with you." Seven said as he pushed the unlock button. "Give Lola your number and we will be in touch. I may need some more of those boxing tips." Seven said just before he extended his hand and smiled. Ball shook his hand and just like that . . . he made first contact.

Chapter Six

Seven's Rah

Seven stared at the diagnosis that Rah's doctor had sent them. He pulled the letter out of his mailbox and as he read the word Terminal, his eyes could not stop watering. It was real. He had always known that his son's time would come, but now that there was an official countdown Seven was sick with grief.

"Dad what's wrong?" Rah asked as he looked up curiously from the homework that sat in front of him. Rah sat wide eyed and curious on top of a barstool at the kitchen island as he waited for his father's response. The dark circles under Li'l Rah's eyes revealed that today hadn't been a good day. He was tired and weak from fighting the cancer cells that were eating him alive and as Seven looked up from the letter he thought, *if my li'l man can be strong, than so can I.*

"I'm good li'l man . . . just got something in my eye," he responded as he folded the paper and put it in his back pocket. "How's that homework coming?" Seven asked.

"Good," Rah responded with a confident nod.

"You holding it down in the classroom? What I tell you about a dumb nigga?" Seven asked.

"A dumb nigga don't make no paper. The vault to the good life is locked down and I can find the key inside these books," Rah responded, repeating the words that Seven had spoken to him a thousand times.

"That's right . . . my main man," Seven complimented as he slapped hands with his son. "What else is going on in school? You got a few young ladies sniffing behind you yet boy?"

"Yep," Li'l Rah said with a smile.

"Yeah?" Seven asked with a chuckle.

"Yeah," Rah confirmed as his bird chest poked out proudly.

Seven walked over to the stove and turned on the burners as he began to pull pots and pans from his cabinets. He removed fresh vegetables from his refrigerator.

"Aww dad can't we have something good for a change . . . like pancakes or something?" Rah asked.

Usually Seven was strict on his son's health and would fix him a well balanced meal for dinner but as he looked at his son who was fighting for his life he thought, *he can have pancakes everyday for the rest of his life.*

"A'ight li'l man. Pancakes it is."

Rah's mouth dropped open in surprise and then a huge smile spread across his young face. He looked up to his father and thought he was the coolest man on the planet, but he was surprised that Seven was being so lenient.

"With chocolate chips?" Rah asked.

"I got you covered," Seven replied as he pulled out the pancake batter. As he made their night time breakfast Seven thought about how to approach his son with the bad news. The next week Rah was due for another round of radiation treatment and also another run of tests. He knew how his little man hated the poking and prodding that came with the tests. The radiation seemed to drain all of the life out of him, but it was necessary. Seven was doing all that he could to keep

Rah alive and unfortunately he had to go through hell to treat the cancer. It was like a game of hide and seek. One month Rah would be doing good and the doctor's would be hopeful that the cancer had gone into remission. But it never failed . . . the next time they went to the doctor the disease would be back wrecking havoc on his son's insides. It always came back and now that the doctor's had put them on a timeline. Seven was trying to prepare himself from the inevitable. He had only lost one other person in his life who had ever meant anything. That tragedy had changed the man that he was, but this new impending one . . . the death of Rah . . . would surely kill him. Just as he wrapped up their pancakes he sat a huge plate in the middle of the table and then fixed them both a serving.

"Thanks dad," Rah said as he began to stuff his face.

"You're welcome li'l man," Seven replied. As he cut up his pancakes he approached the conversation with caution. "You remember Dr. Clark?" he asked.

As if his heart had been deflated Rah dropped his fork, clanking it against his plate and looked up at his father. "I don't want to go back there daddy. I'm tired," Rah said with tears in his eyes.

The sight of Rah's fear broke Seven down on the inside but he couldn't show it.

"I know man, but you have to be strong. Dr. Clark is just trying to make you better. You have to be here to take care of your old man and she is going to help me make that happen."

"No she's not," Rah stated as he reluctantly picked back up his fork. "I'm gonna die."

"What?" Seven asked seriously. He was slightly vexed because he had never informed Rah of the seriousness or the time limit of his condition. "Who told you that Rah?"

"Deandre Richardson at school told me people with cancer all die. He wouldn't let me play hoop with him and his boys because he said that if I touched his basketball he'd catch cancer and die too," Rah said angrily.

"Deandre Richardson huh?" Seven said. He wished that the name he had just dropped didn't belong to a child because he would have definitely paid him a visit, but he knew that children could be mean and he had to remind himself to calm down. "Well, is Deandre a doctor Rah?"

"No," Rah responded.

"So he can't speak intelligently right?" Seven asked.

"Right," Rah responded despondently.

Seven stood and walked around to Rah's side of the table before bending down on one knee so that they were eye to eye. "As long as I'm breathing we are going to fight this together okay? You are going to experience just as much as anybody else in this world . . . cancer or not. That's my word. You hear me?" he asked.

"Yeah I hear you," Rah replied.

"And fuck Deandre Richardson. I bet you he ain't going to the Cleveland and Lakers game this weekend now is he?" Seven asked, pulling the basketball tickets out of his back pocket.

A huge smile erased all of the pain from Rah's face. He had a crazy obsession for basketball and the idea of going to a game distracted him from his current circumstance.

"Nope!" Rah said.

"Matter fact . . . let your whole class know that their going . . . everyone except for Deandre Richardson," Seven stated.

"For real dad?" Rah shouted.

"For real homie," Seven confirmed as he kissed the top of Rah's bald head.

"Thanks daddy, I'ma be the man! You're the best! Fuck Deandre Richardson!"

Seven popped the back of Rah's head gently and responded, "Watch your mouth, boy."

Just as he was about to take his seat he felt the vibration of his phone on his hip. Lola's face popped up on his screen and he immediately answered the call.

"What up?" he asked.

"We should talk about the kid Ball. He's coming to Hazel's tonight. Can you meet me there?" she asked, her angelic voice filling his ear.

"Yeah give me a few. I'm coming from my crib. I'll meet you there," he responded.

Seven stood from the table just as his nanny entered the kitchen. The Latino woman shook her head as she asked, "Oh Rah, what are you eating?"

"Chocolate chip pancakes," he said with a mouthful.

Seven turned his back to his son and reached in the kitchen drawer to retrieve his strap. He concealed it in his waistline before facing Rah. "I've gotta go meet Lola. I'll be back later tonight. You be good a'ight?" he asked.

"A'ight," Rah responded as he pounded his father's fist.

"I love you man."

"I love you too," Rah responded. It was the last words he heard before he left the house, and they were motivation enough to make him want to move wisely. Everything he did was for Rah. His son needed him but little did Rah know . . . Seven needed him just as much.

Seven stood in his office in the back of the bar looking out of his two-sided mirror at the busy patrons who frequented the spot. He could see all that was happening throughout his establishment, and although he was peering out of a window . . . from the patrons' point of view they were looking into a mirror. They never even knew his private office sat on the other side of the wall. He sipped cognac slowly, savoring the dark flavor of the liquor as he checked his Movado watch. He wanted to be observant of the time. Timeliness said a lot about a person's efficiency. He already had it in his mind that if Ball stepped foot inside his bar a minute past 11:30 P.M. then he would not deal with him.

"Looks like he may be late," Seven said as heard his office door open behind him. He didn't need to look. He knew that she was the only person who had the balls to walk into his space without knocking.

"He said he would be here," Lola said as she stood beside Seven, her Prada perfume filling the room. "If he's late. . . . it's a wrap. Tardiness is a habit and I'm not trying to take on another headache. If his ass is dumb enough to be late for this meeting, then he'll be dumb enough to be late on the money and I really don't want to have to get at this guy. He's kinda cute." Lola smirked as she nudged Seven's shoulder. He shook his head from side to side.

"What?" she feigned innocence.

"You about to catch another one up in Lola's web?" he asked.

"Shut up Seven," she said with an eye roll. She focused her eyes out onto the club and noticed Ball walk into the door with five minutes to spare. "He's here."

Seven looked out on the crowd until his eyes fell onto Ball. He noticed the cautious look in Ball's eye and the constant swivel of his neck as he checked his surroundings. Fresh in designer threads he smelled like money and Seven had to give it to him . . . the young dude seemed to have some hustle about him.

"Bring him back," Seven stated as he took a seat in his executive style leather chair. Seven wasn't a friendly nigga and it was rare that he even considered opening up his circle, but he sensed something in Ball. There weren't many hustlers who could afford a front row ticket at a Vegas heavy-weight fight, but Ball was sitting right there . . . amongst the stars as if he belonged. And if he was getting money in Ohio, Seven needed to know about him. If Ball passed all the tests, Seven wouldn't hesitate to give the young man a starting spot on his roster.

Braylon walked into the bar his nerves on edge as he looked around, surveying those around him. Butter-flies filled the pit of his stomach. His usual confidence waned and he felt transparent as if everybody in the joint knew his true intentions. He shook off his appre-hension and adjusted his posture as he made his way inconspicuously through the crowd. He looked around for Lola and quickly spotted her. She stood out in the crowd like a diamond amongst gems. Her bright white smile contrasted off of her dark as night skin as her long legs closed the distance between them.

"I'm glad you could make it," she greeted as she looped her arm inside his, instantly turning him into her escort. It wasn't hard to make niggas comply to her. She switched men like she did handbags, classily dismissing them when they no longer complimented her lifestyle. They were accessories and as she walked through the bar people cleared out of her path. She was a boss bitch and Braylon noted the respect she garnered as people acknowledged her with a head nod as she passed them by. Braylon could tell that she was respected in the streets and silently wondered how a woman had developed so much clout. As they approached Seven's door she knocked this time, wanting to show the utmost respect to Seven in front of Braylon.

"It's open," Seven shouted as Lola walked through the door with Braylon following.

Seven stood from his desk and slapped hands with Braylon in greeting.

"Good to see you again. Have a seat," he said cordially. Braylon took a seat and Seven continued. "You see, what I can't figure out for the life of me is how you flew underneath my radar. You're buying up a lot of real estate and I knew nothing about you." Seven was no fool. He was speaking in code and by real estate he meant kilos of cocaine. "But you're not buying no bullshit houses . . . you're copping prime real estate. The good joints, nah mean? Now real estate is my business. So what I can't understand is why you're not buying from me."

"My realtor gives me them foreclosure prices," Ball replied.

Seven smirked, liking Ball already. There was something about him that Seven respected. He was young and hustling . . . black and driven . . . all qualities that Seven possessed as well.

"I can beat any price, but it depends on the quantity of course. The more properties you buy the better the price will be. My real estate also comes with security. I'm not trying to step on your toes a' nothing, but I want in. If there's money to be made I want to get it and since you already familiar with the Toledo area, I want to bring you in on my team."

Braylon knew that if he was too eager than Seven would back out so he leaned forward as he adjusted the diamond bracelet on his wrist.

"No offense fam, but why would I join a team when I'm doing good with my own thing?"

"Because with my business comes insurance," Seven said. "You won't take any losses."

"Price?" Braylon asked.

Seven loved the back and forth. He could tell that Ball wasn't from where he was from because he didn't fear Seven. Most hustlers would be afraid to haggle with Seven, but Ball took the meeting by the balls and fought for control. Both Seven and Ball knew who the real boss was, and they both knew that at the end of the day Ball would end up working beneath Seven. The negotiating was refreshing. Ball was about his business and his money, which caused Seven to respect him.

Seven smirked. "Reasonable," he responded, referring to the price of his product, but not throwing out a specific number. Seven was smart and there was a mystique about him that drew both men and women in. Men wanted to emulate him and women wanted to be with him. Ball was no different. He was enamored by the enormity of Seven's reign. He had done his research before walking into the bar. Seven wasn't to be fucked with. A modern day gangster . . . Seven was the stuff that legends were made of.

Lola sat silently by Ball's side and she watched him closely. She looked for anxiety, for shade, noting his character. She could read a man like a book. *No closed fists, no clenched jaw . . . he's not nervous. He's maintaining eye contact,* she noted thoroughly in her head. Nothing about Ball's body language was throwing red flags. Even when Seven let silence linger in the air purposefully to rattle Ball, he remained composed. Seven and Lola locked eyes for a split second. That was all it took for Seven to notice the approval in Lola's gaze. She had given him the thumbs up without saying a word.

He trusted Lola's word. She had never steered him wrong before. Ball was a go.

"I need to know a more specific price before I can say yay or nay, nah mean?" Ball asked.

"No you don't," Seven responded. "All you need to know is that those I have chosen to do business with in the past is getting money. They're wealthy. Wifey's happy, kids fed. . . . Are you in or out?"

Ball looked from Lola to Seven and nodded in consent, "I'm in."

The connection had been made.

"Where are you staying?" Seven asked.

"The Hyatt," Ball replied.

"Lola will be in touch," Seven stated as he picked up his business phone and began to dial a number. Lola stood and Ball wasn't quite sure if the meeting was over, but when Seven looked up from his phone call and said, "You're still sitting here?" Ball knew there was nothing left to say.

He got up and headed out of the office feeling as if he had just made the biggest move of his life.

"By the way, I go by Ball. Call me Ball." he said as walked out of the door.

"Room service!"

Braylon sat straight up in his hotel bed and rubbed his eyes as he looked over at the clock that sat on the nightstand. It was 7:00 A.M. and he irritably got out of bed.

"Fucking room service . . . I ain't ordered shit," he grumbled as he crawled out of bed and walked over to the door. He opened the door and to his surprise no one stood on the other side. In place of the voice was a large black duffel bag. Braylon stepped out into the hall and looked from one end to the other, but no one was in sight. He bent down and picked up the bag before carrying it inside his room. He closed the door behind him and then tossed the bag on his bed. He unzipped the bag to find the prettiest bitches he had ever seen. Ten kilo's sat inside, neatly wrapped in clear cellophane.

Dumbfounded he pulled a brick out of the bag. It was uncut. He could tell by the way it sparkled and his hustler's instinct quickly kicked in. *I can make these birds fly,* he thought. It was then that he realized that he was stepping into a league that he was unfamiliar with. He had been getting money, but Seven was on some other shit. He was hustling in a major way. He hadn't even told Seven his room number and the room wasn't registered in his name. Just the fact that Seven was able to locate him told Braylon how large he was and he silently hoped that he didn't get in over his head. He was about to transform into Ball . . . the hustler. He would have to play this role to regain his freedom. In actuality, it was the beginning of the end.

Chapter Seven

Exit Braylon, Enter Ball

Ball let the water cascade down his naked body as he rested his hand on the shower's wall. He was impressed by the recent delivery that he had just gotten. Seven handled his business with swagger and professionalism. Ball was dealing with the upper class in drug distribution at that point. Honestly, he was nervous about stepping into this dirty game on the same side as the law. He stepped out of the shower and was startled when he saw a man standing at the door looking at him.

"Oh shit!" Ball yelled as he almost slipped on the floor. He noticed that it was Dame who had snuck up on him. He never thought he would be so happy to see a cop. He honestly thought Seven had sent one of his goons to kill Ball that quickly.

"What the fuck man?" Ball said as he stood there naked.

"Get on some clothes and meet me in the front. Quick." Dame demanded as he left out. Ball grabbed a robe and headed to the front where Dame waited at the small dinette table.

"What the fuck you sneaking up on me for?" Ball said as he dried his ears with a towel.

"First of all . . . I can do whatever the fuck I want. You are state property until I'm done with your ass. Let's be clear on that." Dame said with a stern tone as he pointed at Ball.

"Whatever. Hold on. I got good news." Balls said as he walked to the closet. He grabbed the duffle bag that Seven had arranged to be dropped off to him and walked to the table where Dame was seated. Ball then emptied the plastic wrapped bricks onto the table.

"Who gave you this?' Dame asked as his eyed looked on in awe.

"Seven did. So I'm done right? I got the drugs, now go arrest his ass and send me on my way," Ball said.

"Seven actually gave you these himself?" Dame asked with skepticism all over his face.

"Well, not exactly. This morning I heard a knock at the door and when I answered this is what I found. But I saw him the previous night and he basically told me that he was going to hit me with the bricks."

"That's not good enough. If we want to put him away for a long time, we have to build a case. This is not going to happen overnight. This is a slow grind that I handpicked you for. You have to get in his circle and move like him. We need to get him to trust you and let you in. This way you can get us to the source. You have a get out of jail free card. You can basically break any law and not worry about getting in trouble. Any law except murder."

"Is that right . . . ?"

"So I want you to do what you do best nigga . . . hustle. I want you to do what you do and don't think about what's at the end of the road. It's either you go all the way in or don't go at all. I don't have to tell you the alternative do I?" Dame asked as he stood up and tossed one of the bricks to Ball. "Jail for a very long time. Think about it." he said just before he left the room, leaving Ball alone to think to himself.

Chapter Eight

Snitching with Benefits

Ball dropped the dope off to Dame at the boxing gym and Dame gave him more money to re-order with. They were about to slowly build a strong case against Seven. Dame brought Ball to the backroom where a young man with a briefcase was waiting for them.

"What the fuck is this?" Ball asked as he stared at the young light-skinned man in front of them. He closely resembled a Hollywood model with his good grade of hair and high yellow skin.

"This is Gary, he's a police officer who is about to go undercover."

"Okay, what does this have to do with me?" Ball asked.

"I want you to introduce him to Seven as a potential buyer. We have never had someone get close to Seven like you have. We need a more experienced person working on the inside." Dame said as he folded his arms and leaned against the wall.

"You got to be kidding me? This nigga?" Ball said with skepticism as he pointed at Gary. He began to look Gary up and down and knew that Seven would sniff him out a mile away. "You trying to get me killed? I can't do that. This nigga ain't been in the streets a day in his life."

"You do not know anything about me nigger," Gary said as he stood up and poked out his chest. Ball couldn't help but to burst out in laughter.

"First of all, it's nigga, not nigger. This is the shit I'm talking about. This nigga ain't street. And you need to sit yo' punk ass down before I pistol whip yo' ass," Ball said with a smile stepping into Gary's face.

"Hold up!" Dame screamed as he stepped in between the two men. "Settle down! And Ball, you ARE going to introduce him to Seven. If not, I'll ship your ass back to prison so fast that your head will spin."

"I can't believe this bullshit. Okay, I'll do it." Ball said after an extended moment of silence. "At least tell me you don't want me to introduce him as Gary. That shit sounds weak."

"No, I go by G-Dog." Gary said proudly in protest. Ball couldn't help but to chuckle.

"Look, your name is G. That G-Dog shit is corny as fuck. And please go get you some new clothes and not none of this bullshit you got on." Ball said as he shook his head and put his hands on his waist. Gary remained silent as he looked down at the clothes he had picked out as street gear.

"Cool. Now come over here and let me show you something." Dame walked over to the table and flipped open the briefcase. He exposed several pieces of platinum and gold jewelry. All of the pieces were shiny and diamond clustered. Ball immediately knew they were real and expensive by the way it looked.

"If you're going to play the part . . . you have to look the part. These are pieces that were confiscated from drug dealers over the years. Raids, seized items, and evidence inventory had stockpiled over the years. Take your pick." Dame said as he stepped back and let them pick their jewelry. Gary instantly went for the biggest piece in the briefcase. He grabbed a platinum chain with a diamond encrusted Jesus head. The piece was custom made and was one of a kind. He put it around his neck and looked down in pure admiration. He always fantasized about wearing one and he finally had the opportunity to put on a chain worth more than his house.

"I am going to take this," Ball said as he grabbed a modest platinum Rolex with a diamond front. It wasn't too flashy, but it looked like money. It was a perfect fit for him.

"Great. Remember, it's a marathon not a sprint. We have to build a case on this man and take him down. Let's take our time and try to get deep in his organization." Dame said as he closed the briefcase and walked out. "Have a goodnight gentleman. And remember, I'm always watching." He said as he exited the room, leaving the two men alone.

Ball looked at the corny dude next to him and shook his head, knowing that he wasn't fit to play the part. Fucking around with Dame's people was sure to get him killed. He would never introduce anybody to Seven again. He was going to do it his way from that point on. Period.

Chapter Nine

New York State of Mind

Club Karma was rocking. Seven and his crew were in the building in the VIP section. It was a particularly special night. It was Lola's birthday and everyone in the city came out to show love to the first lady. The Goon Squad along with Seven and Lola, posted in the roped off section in the rear. All eyes were on their section but no one could come close to the infamous crew. The goons posted front and center making sure no one crossed into their section. The bass thumped through the speakers and it was a couple of ticks before midnight. Lola danced by herself with her hands in the air as her favorite song came through the speakers. A bottle of Rose' was in her hand and she drank the thousand-dollar champagne like it was water.

Ball sat at the bar and sipped on a vodka and cranberry, periodically glancing at the VIP section. He got wind of the party and under Dame's order, was forced to go and mingle. Ball pulled out a wad of money and peeled off a fifty to pay for his drink. He told the waitress to keep the change as he turned his back on the bar and scoped out the place. Ball noticed men and women's heads beginning to turn as a woman walked by. She had the biggest ass Ball had ever seen in his life. Her thin waist made her look like drawn cartoon figure, rather than a real person. Her body was simply amazing. She wore a tight fitting dress that hugged her figure, leaving nothing to the imagination. She wore red stilettos and a short bob hairstyle similar to that of actress Nia Long's. Every time she took a step, her weight shifted from one plump butt cheek to the other. Her juicy behind jiggled every time her foot hit the pavement and the men drooled over her as she made her way to the bar. She approached and stood right next to Ball, ordering a drink.

"What's up daddy?" she asked as she looked over at Ball and smiled, showing her pretty smile. Her smooth, brown complexion and dimples solidified her beauty and Ball was definitely impressed.

"What up," he answered coldly as he looked her up and down and then back at the dance floor.

"Nice watch." She added as she glanced down at the diamond encrusted Rolex. It seemed as if her eyes lit up when she saw the jewelry on his arm. She couldn't hide it. Ball caught on.

"Thanks." Ball said uninterested. The girl could feel his unwelcoming vibe and she quickly jerked her head and rolled her eyes.

"Your loss," she said as she got her drink and walked away. Ball smiled and shook his head at her ignorance. The word gold-digger oozed from her personality and Ball saw right through her. He didn't want any part of her. Zoey was the only girl that was on his mind, so hooking up with a chick was the last thing on his mind.

"Shorty got a fat ass though," Ball said to himself as he watched her walk away. His eyes followed her as she walked to the corner of the room where two guys were leaning against the wall in black hoodies. She whispered something to one of them and walked away. Ball's antennas instantly went up, but he dismissed it when a tap on his shoulder took his attention. It was Lola.

"Yo, what's up homeboy?" she asked holding an extra bottle in her hand.

"Hey Lola," Ball said as he smiled and looked her up and down. Although she dressed casually, wearing skinny jeans and a small jacket, she still had sex appeal.

"I got your text. You done with them joints already?" Lola said referring to the bricks that she hit him with.

"Yeah, I'm on the last joint. I need to re-up," Ball said confidently as he took a sip of his drink.

"Yo, come up to VIP with us. I saw you over here looking lonely," Lola joked as she unleashed her smile. She handed him a bottle and led him back to their section. Ball bobbed his head to the music and approached the booth Seven and a couple of ladies were sitting at.

"Look who I found in the crowd," Lola said as she slid in the booth next to Seven.

"The new kid on the block," Seven said as he smiled and extended his hand. He slapped hands with Ball, greeting him.

"What's the word?" Ball asked as he scoped the VIP scene. The club had roped off the whole section for Seven and his crew. Only Goon Squad was allowed. Of course, a couple of special females were granted access. Bottles were flowing and they owned the club.

"Just celebrating my little sister's birthday," Seven said as he downed the rest of his champagne.

"Happy birthday, Lola B!" One of the goons yelled as he held up a bottle. He also let a couple of girls into their section. Lola stood up and whispered to Seven that she was about to use the restroom. Lola stood up and headed toward the restroom while the goon unhooked the velvet rope and stepped to the side, letting the stampede of stallions gain entrance. All eyes were on the girl in the red dress with the gigantic ass. She was the same girl that had approached Ball just minutes ago.

Seven leaned over toward Ball and said, "I hear you making them things move. Your whole supply gone in seven days; I see you out here," Seven said as he nodded his head in approval. Just as Ball was about to respond, the girl in the red dress slid next to Seven. Seven's attention immediately diverted to the voluptuous woman who had just sat down.

"How you doing, mister?" the woman asked.

"I'm good, ma. I saw you from up here. You got the whole club's attention," Seven said as he downed another shot of liquor that was in front of him. Normally he wouldn't drink that much but he was determined to celebrate on behalf of Lola's special day. Ball looked toward the corner of the room and saw the two men that the girl in the red dress whispered to, watching closely. He instantly knew something was up. *Look like stick-up kids to me*, he thought as he let the situation unfold.

"Hi, I'm Kim," the girl said to Seven.

"I'm Seven. Nice dress." He said with a slight grin.

"I hear you run this town," Kim said to Seven as she placed her hand on his lap.

"Is that right?" Seven answered in a slurred voice. The drinks had him feeling good at that point.

"Yeah that's right. I have been watching you all night. I'm not going to lie . . . you make me horny as hell," She said cutting straight to the point.

"Damn baby. You don't hold any punches do you?" Seven asked as he sat up and looked down at her thick hips.

"Naw, not really. I'm from BK and we don't beat around the bush. I'm here for the weekend visiting my cousin and I'm trying to have a goodtime," she said as she licked her lips while looking deep into Seven's eyes. Her sex appeal was undeniable and she had mastered the art of seduction. She slipped her hand over to Seven's croch area. He quickly removed her hand, but she went right back to it. Persistence was the key.

"Brooklyn huh? You are a long way from home sweet-heart," Seven said as he felt the woman palm his man-hood as she begin to stroke it. He wanted to remove her hand but it felt so good. His thin Armani slacks didn't make it any better. He felt his manhood began to grow.

"Everybody saying you the man around here, and I only fuck with the best. I want to taste you," She said as she inched closely to him, putting her lips on his ear. She let out a slight moan and licked his lobe, sending chills up his back.

"Damn, ma," Seven said as he closed his eyes. He had women throwing themselves at him all the time, but with the influence of the liquor and the woman's skills . . . he was weak.

"Let's talk somewhere a little more private," she re-quested as she slid from underneath the table and stood up. Her big juicy behind was in direct eyesight of Seven and it only enticed him more. She wiggled to pull down her dress over her hips and it was like she was moving in slow motion. Seven's joint instantly got rock hard and he slid from underneath the table also.

"Tell Lola I'll be right back," he said to Ball as he smiled and winked. Ball smiled back as he looked at the girl's body. Seven pulled the girl through the back entrance where his crew had parked. Ball looked over at the dudes posted on the back wall as they exited through the front door almost simultaneously with Kim and Seven. He knew something was up. The rest of the goons were so busy partying and bullshitting, they didn't notice what was about to go down. They didn't even notice that Seven had slipped away. Ball was from the East Coast so he could spot a stick-up plan from a mile away. It was the advantage of having a New York state of mind.

Seven watched as Kim played with her clit while sucking him off. He threw his head back in pleasure while sitting in the back seat of his spacious Cadillac truck. The way she used her tongue was nothing short of amazing. She took him in her mouth and circled her tongue around his throbbing shaft. The sexy sound of her wet box getting popped by her fingers was driving Seven crazy. She was a certified freak and he had never seen anything like it. She began to move her hips in a grinding motion and she inserted her two fingers inside her vagina.

"Oh my God," Seven said as looked down at her neatly shaven vagina.

"I wanna feel this big dick inside of me," she whispered as she sat up and began to stroke his manhood. She pulled her dress over her head, revealing her small perky breasts. Her nipples stuck straight out like little fingers and Seven instantly began to suck them. Kim straddled Seven as she reached for her purse. She pulled out a condom and put it on Seven's manhood. She then removed the gun that was on his waist.

"This thing is poking me," she said as she tossed it in the front seat. That must have been the signal, because as soon as she tossed it, the back doors flew open taking them by complete surprise. It was one of the two men from inside the club. It was a setup. Seven couldn't believe this was happening. The girl quickly hopped off his lap and pulled down her dress.

"Aggh!" she yelled as looked around in confusion.

"You know what time it is homeboy! Take us to the bricks and the money." The masked man said as he held the gun to Seven's head. Seven began to laugh as he put his hands up.

"Do you know who the fuck I am?" he said as he shook his head from side to side, knowing that the youngsters didn't know what they were getting themselves into.

"Shut the fuck up," one of the masked robbers said as he struck Seven across the face with the butt of his gun. Seven instantly grabbed his nose as it began to bleed. The robber pulled Seven and the girl out of the car. Seven was thrown onto the ground and the masked man stood over him.

"Take me to the spot or I'ma blow your bitch's brains out and then yours," he said. A Jimmy truck pulled up and the door opened. It was the other guy from the club.

"Yo, let's put him in the trunk and get the fuck outta here," he said as he got out of the trucwk with his hands up. "Hurry the fuck up!" he added. He never saw who was creeping up behind him.

"Thank you very much," Ball said as he relieved him of his gun, while digging his own into the stick-up kid's neck. "Drop that homeboy or I will blow this mu'fuckas brains out." Ball said as he looked over at the other assailant that had a gun to Seven. Ball instantly saw the shaking hand of the gunman.

Ball pulled back the hammer of his gun and calmly said, "Now I'ma give you one more chance. If you don't let my man go, I'ma dead this nigga right here. One . . ." before he could even get to the next number Seven grabbed the gun from the man and put his own gun in his face.

"Bitch-ass nigga," Seven said as he struck the man across his face. Ball pushed the man he had been holding at gunpoint on the ground next to his partner. He and Seven stood over them with guns in their faces.

"Bitch, you get down there too," Ball said as he pushed Kim onto the ground. Seven looked at Ball like he was crazy for pushing Kim, thinking she had nothing to do with it.

"That bitch set it up. I saw the whole thing," Ball said as he caught Seven up to speed.

"Oh, yeah?" Seven said as he looked at the woman who laid in front of them speechless. Seven pulled back the hammer of his gun and pointed it at the woman. Ball instantly got nervous and grabbed Seven's arm.

"No, not here. There's cameras all around this mu'fucka," he said trying to avoid catching a murder charge.

"Yeah, you right," Seven said as he looked around. Just as he was about to say something else, Lola and his goons bust out of the back door with their guns drawn.

"Y'all a day late and a dollar short," Seven said through clenched teeth. He was furious that his team didn't catch the caper. "If it wasn't for this nigga, I would be in a trunk right now. Put these niggas in the car. Dumb mu'fuckas!" He said angrily as he put his gun in his waist and walked away. He threw his arm around Ball and walked him to his truck.

"Roll with me for a minute." He said as he shook his head in disbelief. And just like that it was over.

"What are they going to do with them?" Ball asked as he looked back to see the goons stuffing the stick-up crew into their own trunk; all three of them.

"They're just going to smack em' up a little. This isn't the first time niggas have tried to test me. I have to stay on my shit. If it wasn't for you and your alertness . . ." Seven stopped and looked into Ball's eyes. "I don't wanna even think about it. Let's go have breakfast. . . . on me." He said as the jumped into the truck. Seven knew that Ball was a great asset to his team and he needed someone sharp like him. It was the beginning of something real.

Chapter Ten

Bad Boys Move in Silence

Seven and Ball sat at the twenty-four hour breakfast spot just down the highway. Lola sat next to Seven as they chatted over steak and eggs. As Seven cut his steak with a knife and fork, he looked at Ball.

"You know I owe you for what you did tonight?" Seven said in modesty.

"It ain't nothing. I saw that shit from a mile away. Honestly, your lil niggas should have been on that." Ball said as he whispered across the table. He looked over at Seven's goons seated at the table a couple feet away from them. Just as Ball was about to speak again, he felt his phone buzz. He looked down and saw that it was a text from Dame. The text read: "G is a block away. Plug him in." Ball clenched his jaw and hated that he had to deal with that clown. He instantly smiled and shook his head. "Chick's be hounding a nigga," he said as he put the phone on his hip.

"I fuck with you the long way. I really like the way you move. I know you got your own thing going on out of town, but if you want you should come fuck with me for a while. Join the team and feel it out, ya know," Seven propositioned as he put the steak in his mouth.

"I wouldn't have it any other way," Ball said as he nodded his head in approval.

"You should come join us for Sunday dinner. It's something that has turned in to a ritual for us. We get money together, but we break bread together also." Seven said showing a gesture of loyalty.

"I appreciate that. I will be there," Ball said. As Ball put a forkful of food into his mouth he saw an all-black E-class Mercedes Benz pull up. The luxury car sat on shiny rims and caught everyone's attention within eyesight. Just as Dame promised, Gary stepped out of the car. He had a female on his arm and Ball instantly knew that she probably was an undercover too. He turned his head trying not to give so much attention to him. Gary walked in and it was hard not to notice the blinging chain that hung from his neck. The lights bounced off of the sparkling diamonds and seemed as if it illuminated the room. He was definitely shining. G took a table across the room from them as Seven and Ball continued to engage in small talk. Ball could feel Gary looking over at them and he tried his best to avoid meeting his gaze. Unfortunately, one of Seven's goons noticed that Gary was staring also. They slyly clicked their gun off safety and walked over to Seven. The goon bent down over the table as whispered to Seven. "Ol' boy across the room keeps looking over here. Want me to go over there and see what's on his mind?"

"Who? The cat over there with the female?" Seven asked as he discreetly glanced over at Gary. Ball didn't even bother looking over there and knew that G was an amateur. He was about to get himself killed. Seven nodded and the goon immediately went over there. They watched as the goon went over and had a word with G. Moments later, the goon came back and looked at Ball.

"My man said he know you," the goon announced.

Ball looked over and G threw his hands up as if he had seen an old friend. Ball whispered under his breath and squinted his eyes as if he wasn't familiar with G.

"You know this nigga?" Seven asked as G stood from his table and made his way over.

"Yo, no disrespect. Just saw an old friend over here." G said as stood over their table. He reached his hand out to Ball, and Ball looked at Seven who had no expression on his face. He looked back at G and reluctantly shook his hand.

"Oh, what up G. Long time no see," Ball said as he eyed G and his corny demeanor. "What you doing in this neck of the woods?" Ball asked.

"Just in town for a couple of weeks checking out new real estate. The prices for property high as hell back home. Feel me? And plus, my girl grew up here." G said as he looked back and pointed at the girl who waited for him at the table. Ball nodded as he listened to the fast-talking G. Just to stop him from talking anymore, Ball cut him off.

"Yo Seven, this is my man G. He in the same business as us. I used to fuck with him back home," He said as he reluctantly vouched for the clown that stood before them.

"What's up gangster." Seven said coldly, almost being sarcastic. "Nice chain," Seven said as looked at the iced out piece G had on. Seven then he stood up and motioned for his team to roll out. He wasn't even done with his food and his action seemed abrupt. Ball looked in confusion as the whole crew began to exit the spot. Seven reached into his pocket and peeled off a hundred dollar bill and tossed it on the table.

"See you tomorrow, Ball. Lola will call you with the directions. Nice to meet you, P." Seven said with a smile as he reached out and shook G's hand.

"It's G," Gary corrected as he shook his hand.

"My apologies," Seven said while Lola and the Goon Squad laughed at the inside joke. Within seconds, Seven and the crew was out of the door and gone. G stood there dumbfounded with his hands out wondering what he did wrong.

"What did I say?" G asked as he looked at Ball in confusion.

"Nothing man. You wouldn't understand," Ball said as he threw his napkin down and shook his head in disbelief. He did not want G to blow this for him. His freedom was at stake and Ball had to let Dame know that his method was not going to work. He only hoped that Seven didn't stop dealing with him. *This stupid clown is throwing salt in the game. I have to tell Dame that I have to do this my way, or I can't do it at all,* he thought to himself as he left a twenty on the table for the waitress.

"Man, take me back to my car." He said to G as he continued to shake his head and go toward the exit.

"This nigga could have gotten me killed. He has fed written all over him. The nigga is soft Dame. Point blank!" Ball said as he paced the floor at the gym. Dame stood there with his hands in his pockets as he let Ball break it down. "First, this nigga walks in the spot with all this flashy shit looking like a clown. With the loud jewelry and fancy car, he was screaming for attention. Niggas who are really getting money, hate attention. The loudest person in the room is the weakest person in the room, believe that! Bad boys move in silence." Ball expressed as he finally stopped and looked at Dame with his hands on his hips.

At first Dame was going to contest, but he understood that Ball knew how to move with sharks. He had
to trust Ball's judgment and let him do it his way. He
knew that by attempting to put G into Seven's realm, it
could put the whole operation at risk. "You're right. I
am going to let you do it your way. I'm going to let you
get in deep without any input." Dame agreed. Ball nodded his head in approval, relieved that he didn't have to
deal with G anymore.

"My way this time? No more fake-ass gangsters on
board?" Ball asked.

"Yeah, you got it. There's just one more thing. That
dinner you were telling me about. The one he invited
you to . . ."

"Yeah, what about it?" Ball asked as he frowned up,
knowing that Dame had something up his sleeve.

"I need you to place these bugs in a couple spots." He
said as he pulled out three little gadgets that resembled
silver buttons.

"What the fuck! You want me to put bugs in his house.
You tripping man."

"Don't forget who's the fucking boss. You work
for me, not the other way around," Dame said as he
grabbed Ball's hand and slammed the bugs into his
palm. "Leave these in spots were conversations take
place. Like the living room, the bedroom, and even in
his car. Place them under a table or somewhere not vis-
ible," Dame said as he stared at Ball intensely.

"Fine!" Ball agreed as he spun around on his heels
and exited out the backdoor.

I hate that mu'fucka, Ball thought as he jumped into
his car and pulled off. He headed back to his hotel with
a whole lot to think about.

Chapter Eleven

Dead End

"Lord, I ask you to protect us all and have compassion for our enemies. Although we do unholy things, we are asking for your loving hand to guide us as we maneuver through this concrete jungle. We are on the path to you but until then we have to get this money. God please have mercy on our souls. Amen," Seven said as he sat at the head of the dinner table where Lola, Ball, and his goons sat. Everyone hands were connected as they said "Amen" in unison and sat over the piping hot food that was prepared by Seven's maid. Rah, Seven's son was also at the table amongst adults and Ball watched closely at how Seven catered to his son. He immediately could sense the bond that they shared. Seven loved his son unconditionally. Ball wanted to ask Seven about the absence of Rah's mother, but brushed off the notion not wanting to intrude. Seven's crew was full of deadly killers and dealers, but every Sunday they all would sit down together like family and break bread together. This is the reason why Seven's regime was strong and almost impossible to penetrate. He embraced all members of his inner circle and had no mercy on his enemies and Ball was learning the true meaning of loyalty. He watched how Seven respected everyone in the crew. He didn't look down on anyone and paid attention to detail. Ball remained quiet as chatter and the sounds of silverware scraping the plates as they all dug in.

"I got an A on English paper!" Rah said to his father as his eyes lit up at his own accomplishment.

"Again?" Seven said as his eyes got big and a smile formed on his face. "Y'all hear that? My boy gon be a writer someday! He be killing them English tests! I have a little genius right here," Seven announced as he rubbed the top of Rah's head. Seven began to clap and everybody followed suit as they gave the young boy an ovation. Rah smiled from ear to ear and it was pure joy in his heart.

"On another note, I want to officially welcome Ball to the team." Seven said as he raised his cup in the air. Everyone, including Ball raised their glass while all eyes were on Seven. "This is to a beautiful friendship and more money than we can spend." Seven said as he raised his glass a tad higher and then took a drink of the wine. Everyone took a drink and Ball smiled and nodded his head as he looked at Seven. Seven had his reservations about Ball, but gave him the benefit of the doubt because he was sharp enough to save his life the night before. He did question Ball's judgement of character. The clown that he introduced him to the night before had him leery. Nevertheless, Seven took a liking to Ball and wanted him on his team. So he shook off the bad notion he had and embraced him . . . temporarily.

"Yo, but ya' man. That nigga suspect. It's something up with that cat. Believe that." Seven said, believing he should drop a gem on his newly acquired soldier.

**

Ball was about to say something back but all chaos broke loose. The loud sound of glass breaking startled everyone as small particles of glass flew everywhere on to everyone. The front glass was shattered and a brick came flying through it. Everyone ducked for cover and hit the floor while grabbing their guns that rested on their waists. Seven instantly grabbed his son and shielded him as he tackled him to the floor and put his hand over his young son's head. Moments later the sound of automatic weapons began to thunder and it began to rain bullets. Bullets flew through the house non-stop, making the walls like Swiss cheese. After thirty seconds of nonstop firing, a silence filled the air and the sounds of screeching tires erupted, echoing through the night's air. After a moment of gasps and screams, things died down and Seven stood up and checked his son who was crying.

"Is everyone okay?" he asked as he brushed the glass off of his shoulder. Rah was crying as he lay on the ground in a fetal position, not knowing what was going on. Everyone responded and no one was hit.

"You're okay big man. Don't worry," he said as he embraced him and slowly rubbed his back. Seven's jaws were clenched so tightly, it seemed as if he would break his teeth. He was boiling with anger. The thought that someone had the audacity to disrespect his home had him on edge. Maria rushed in from the kitchen speaking Spanish, obviously in fear.

"Maria, take him to the back and stay there!" He said as he kissed the top of Rah's head. After a small nudge, Rah ran into Maria's arms and they both disappeared into the back. Immediately, Seven reached into his holster and pulled out his chrome .45-caliber pistol. His goons rushed outside, only to see nothing and hear crickets. Ball stood next to Seven as he breathed heavily and possessed a fire in his eyes that Ball had never witnessed before. Seven wanted blood. He calmed himself and looked over at Lola who was brushing glass off of her shoulder.

"You good Lola?" Seven asked as he put his hands on his hips and shook his head in disgust.

"Yeah, I'm fine," She responded.

Ball looked at Lola and breathed heavily as he tried to grasp what had just happened.

"What the fuck is going on?" Ball asked in confusion.

"I don't know. But I tell you one thing I do know," Seven said just before he paused and looked Ball in the eye. "Someone is going to pay for this." He said with confidence and he headed to the back to his son. It was time for him to relocate. He was dealing with an invisible enemy; the absolute worst kind you could have.

Ball was dead sleep in his bed as the morning sun rays began to beam through the cracks of the blinds. The sounds of birds chirping filled the air as Ball laid there peacefully. He was awake but he hadn't yet opened his eyes. However, the feeling of someone standing over him, made him peek. Ball opened his eyes and saw the barrel of a .40 cal pointed directly in his face. Lola held the gun as Seven stood next to her with his hands slid into his expensive Armani slacks.

"What the fuck!" Ball yelled as he was taken totally by surprise.

"Wake yo' punk ass up," Lola said as she dug the barrel of her gun into Ball's forehead. She wore her hair braided tightly to the back and a silencer was attached at the end of her gun. Seven watched patiently as Ball slowly sat up with his hands up in surrender.

"What's going on? I can explain," Ball said as he began to see his life flash before his eyes. The sensation of the metal against his skin sent chills up his body.

"No need to explain. You're a snitch and well. . . . you gotta die." Seven said calmly. "Do your thing babygirl. Show him how we get down," Seven instructed Lola as he turned around and started to walk toward the door. Ball tried to explain, but his pleas fell on deaf ears as a single shot rang out. Instantly, Ball's brains spattered all over the headboard. Ball never saw it coming; now all he saw was black.

Suddenly, the sound of buzzing rang in the brains he had left. Buzz, Buzz, Buzz. . . .

Ball woke up to a buzzing phone that sat on the night stand. He had just experienced a horrifying nightmare and his body was drenched in sweat. Goosebumps were all over his arms as he looked around in terror. The phone danced across the surface each time it vibrated. It was a text from Lola. It simply read: *Dinner tonight. Meet me at Hazel's at 6 o' clock. Come through back door*. Ball sat up and looked at the clock. It was noon and he had overslept big time. He got up and instantly jumped in the shower. As he let the water hit his face, he began to think about Zoey and how life would be if he hadn't gone to see Ralphie that night. The scenario played over and over in his mind as he let the strong streams of water give his body a slight massage. He knew that before long, he would go see Ralphie and get revenge for what he had done. But first he had to handle his business so he could stay free.

It was Sunday and Hazel's was closed for business. However, the place was semi-full from people from the community. Although Seven moved dope through the area, he was what you called the problem solver. On Sundays, he kept his door open and gave people in the community a chance to speak with him. Seven ran the city and everyone knew it. If someone had a problem, they didn't go to the police; they went to Seven.

Seven sat in his back office with a cigar in his mouth and a small glass of cognac beside him. He started at the teary eyed woman who sat in front of him. Lola stood to the left of him and listened with her arms crossed. She was a single mom who was having trouble paying her rent. She was two months behind and her ends just weren't meeting as planned. She lived in the housing projects that sat in the middle of the city and also one of the main hotspots for Seven's drug business.

"Lillie, you still fuck with that shit?" Seven asked, knowing that she once had a bad heroin addiction back in the day.

"No Seven, I promise. I haven't touched any dope in almost a year. I'm clean." Lillie pleaded as she wiped away the tears on her cheek. Seven remained silent and just stared at Lillie, trying to detect any malice in her eyes. Seven put his cigar down, stood up, and walked around his desk. He leaned on the edge of his desk and stood directly in front of Lillie. She cried as all of her burdens weighed heavy on her soul. She had five young kids at home and she had nowhere else to go. The state assistance she was receiving wasn't enough to keep her out of financial turmoil.

"Lillie, wipe your eyes." Seven said as he handed her a box of tissues that sat at the edge of his desk. He gently grabbed her by her shoulders and lifted her to her feet. He put his arm around her shoulders and walked her to the exit while talking to her patiently.

"Everything is going to be okay. Lola is going to set you up real nice. You don't have to pay rent anymore. I will take care of that. Now, I'ma need your apartment from time to time, ya' know? Let one of my youngins' use your stove sometimes. When the kids are at school, we are going to need you to help package up a couple things, feel me? This way, you can keep a little money in your pocket." Seven said as he gave her his charming smile.

"Seven, Thank you! Thank you so much. I will not let you down," Lillie said as she grabbed his hand and kissed it in appreciation. Lola then walked over and escorted her out. Lillie was thanking Seven all the way out of the door. Seven shook his head as he walked back over to his desk. He heard a knock at the back exit that was attached to his office. He knew it was someone in his crew because no one came in that way. He stepped to the door and opened it. Ball was on the other side of the door waiting.

"Right on time," Seven said as he looked down at his watch. Seven stepped to the side and let Ball come in.

"What's good? Lola told me to meet here," Ball said as took a seat.

"Want a glass of cognac?" Seven asked as he picked up his glass and took a sip.

"Yeah, I will take one," Ball responded. Seven walked over to his mini bar and poured Ball a double shot. He handed it to Ball as he studied Ball's movements. He was trying to see if he sensed any snake in Ball. Lola was just returning to the office as Seven made his way around his desk. He picked up the newspaper that was in front of him and tossed it in front of Ball. Just as the paper hit the desk, Lola had a gun to the back of Ball's neck.

"Read that!" Seven yelled sternly as his mood switched from calm to irate within milliseconds. Ball was taken by surprised and looked down at the paper.

"Cop found dead. Lynched," The headline read.

"So you a fed, huh? Your little friend you tried to introduce me to was a cop. You thought I wouldn't see through that bullshit?" Seven asked. He felt insulted that Ball would even think that he would fall for it.

"Yo, I didn't know. I know that nigga from back home. He used to get those things from me." Ball said nervously as he tried to plead for his life.

"I knew he was a cop as soon he came in. Shit . . . he even walked like one." Seven said as he stood up and expressed his anger.

"Yo, I swear to God. I did not know. You gotta believe me." Ball said.

"The clown ass nigga even had on one of my old goon's chain. That chain was custom made. How do I know? Because I bought it for him, before he got locked up on drug charges a few years back. I know it was the chain the feds confiscated because it's the only one in the world. One of one, homeboy!" Seven explained. Ball instantly thanked God that he passed on the chain and it made him wonder about the Rolex that he currently had on.

"You have to believe me! I didn't know that bitch-ass nigga was a pig. If I knew . . . I would rocked that nigga to sleep my damn self!" Ball shot back with fire in his eyes. Ball honestly forgot that he was undercover and spoke truthfully as he pleaded for his life. Seven stared long and hard as he slowly paced back and forth with his hands in his Armani slacks. Seven then went into his pocket and pulled out a chain. It was the same chain that G had worn. He placed it on top of the article and smiled at Ball.

"That nigga sleeping. You understand me? That's what we do to snakes," Seven said.

"If he was a cop, that's good. I never knew. I wish that nigga a thousand deaths!" Ball screamed.

Seven looked at Lola and then back at Ball. Something was telling him that he made a mistake. There was something about Ball that was authentic and Seven took notice to it. So much tension was in the air, you could cut it with a knife. Lola stood behind Ball ready to shoot on command, and Seven went back and forth in his mind. Ball sat there with his teeth clenched, awaiting his destiny. Lola glanced over at Seven and then shook her head, signaling that they shouldn't kill him. She believed that he was telling the truth. Seven valued Lola's opinion, so he nodded, signaling her to take the gun off of him.

"We just had to be sure," Seven said as he walked around to his desk chair and sat down. He picked up his cigar and took a pull. Ball didn't want to show it, but he was nervous as ever. He thought for sure he was a goner.

"There is nothing fake about me. I'm just trying to get to the money. Nothing more, nothing less. And if you put a gun to my head again . . . you better kill me." Ball said in a threat. Seven respected Ball's gangster.

"I respect that. But I had to make sure. It was too much smoke around the situation." Seven said.

"Come on. Let's get to the money," Lola said as she smiled and patted him on the shoulder.

Ball smiled back, but deep inside he was nervous as hell. He played it off as he took a sip of his drink, knowing that he had just dodged a bullet.

Seven flipped through the pages of the paper and pointed to another article. "This is what we're about. Family over everything. Nobody goes against the family," Seven said as he tapped the headline which read, "Two men and a woman found slain on the northside of

Columbus." Ball instantly knew that Seven had cleaned up the robbers that had tried him the other night. At that moment, Ball realized how treacherous Seven was. He ran the streets with an iron fist and Ball just witnessed that first hand. Ball was about to get in deep with a real life gangster. Seven spun in his chair, signaling that he was done talking to Ball. The smoke circles seemed to come out of thin air as Seven puffed his cigar and thoughts of accepting a new member on his team danced around on his brain.

"See you guys tonight at dinner," Seven said. With that, Lola motioned for Ball to follow her out the back door. She was about to take him to the trap.

The halls reeked of piss and the busted lights vaguely illuminated the long hallway inside the project housing. Ball followed Lola as they headed to the fifth floor, taking the stairs. Three members from the Goon Squad trailed them as Lola prepared to give Ball a tour of the main money spot. They reached the fifth floor and Lola knocked on door number 552 in a rhythmic pattern. Moments later, the sound of deadbolts clicking echoed throughout the hallway and seconds later Ball was welcomed to the trap.

Ball couldn't believe his eyes as he walked into the door. The open spaced looked like a studio rather than an apartment. Five walls had been knocked down, connecting all of the apartments together. Rows of tables were lined up as females weighed and carefully bagged up heroin. A goon stood guard by the door with a loaded shotgun for security. Every single person in the room acknowledged Lola as she walked the floor. Ball could sense the power that Lola possessed. Her direct affiliation with Seven gave her a status in the streets. Ball scanned the room in awe as he took in the fully functioning trap spot. Everyone was busy either cutting, weighing, or bagging the raw. He couldn't believe his eyes. The strong odor hit him like a tons of bricks. The air conditioner was blaring so the temperature would stay low. The dope had to stay in a cool place so it wouldn't go bad and also to give it a longer life.

"So this is where the magic happens." Lola said as she walked through the spacious spot. Ball looked around at the naked girls and soaked it all in. "This is where they cut it. Bossman doesn't let them cut it more than twice. Our shit isn't stepped on. We want to give the streets the strongest product possible. The difference between good heroin and bad heroin is in the mix. We've got the best mix." Lola explained to him the orders of actions and then led him to the back of the room were two older men sat. They were the testers of the heroin. This position usually didn't stay filled long. If the product was too strong, it usually ended in a drug overdose. Fiends were in line to grab the position as a tester. Even though their lives were at stake, users didn't care. They just saw the opportunity to receive free dope and took the risk. Ball laughed as he saw one of the men in a dope-fiend lean while sitting in a fold up chair. His head was dropping down to his knees in a nod and he would then bounce back up and do the same routine again.

"After the product is packaged up, we drop the packages out this window," Lola said as she waved Ball over and encouraged him to look down. Ball peeked down five stories and saw a couple of goons sitting on the steps. "Once they get the packages they take it to the runner. The runner takes it to another spot and that's where distribution starts."

Ball was impressed. They had the hustling game down to a science.

"Damn," Ball said in amazement as he looked down and around.

"We are going to set you up on the other side of town in our less active areas and see what you can do." Lola said as she crossed her arms and looked Ball intensely in his eyes. Her piercing stare was rough and sexy all at once and Ball took notice.

She sexy than a mu'fucka, Ball thought as he took in all the information. "Yo, put together a four piece for my man and take it to the spot," Lola ordered as she headed toward the exit. "Your bag will be waiting for you at your new spot." Lola said as she nodded at the goon by the door so he could let them back out.

"This is the main spot. Seven rarely comes up here. That's why the feds can't touch him. He never deals with the dope directly; always through me or a hench-man," Lola explained to Ball.

"So everyone is working for a man they never see?" Ball asked trying to get a better understanding.

"That's right. If nobody can point him out as the head of the operation, the feds have no case. Of course the feds know Seven moves weight in this city. But the question is . . . can they prove it?" Lola said as she broke the game down to him. Ball then realized why Dame needed an inside informant for Seven. He had a flawless operation and the only way he could be taken down was by a snitch. The city embraced him so it would have to be an outsider that took him down. Ball just hated that he would have to be the outsider to do it.

They walked back outside and headed out of the projects. Now it was time for Ball to show and prove what he could do with the plug. As Ball staggered back so he could catch a glimpse of Lola's juicy behind, he wondered what made her so gangster, so cold, and so mysterious. It was like she came from a different planet. But like everyone, she had a story.

"So how did you hook up with Seven?" Ball asked trying to get to know more about the intriguing woman that was introducing him to the top shelf of hustling. They got into the car and Lola closed her eyes and threw her head back, digging deep into her memory.

Chapter Twelve
1994: Bunkie Green's Daughter

"Momma wake up!" Lola said as she smacked her mother's face. The small bathroom was tight as Lola tried to maneuver her mother off the toilet and into the tub so she could spray her with water. Her young ten year old eyes had witnessed a lot of pain and trying to wake her mother from a dope fiend lean seemed to be an everyday ritual. Lola came home from school and once again found her mother in the same position on the toilet with a syringe hanging out of her arm. "'Come on ma. Let's get in the shower," Lola said as she pulled the needle out of her and threw her mother's arm around her shoulder. Her mother, Teri, was a small framed woman. She had to be 120 pounds and that was soaking wet. Lola struggled as she placed her mother in the tub and positioned her upright where her face could catch the water from the shower head.

"Come on girl. Wake up," a young Lola said as she reached over and turned on the cold water. Her heart beat in anticipation as the water began to hit her mother's face. She hoped that her mother did not over-dose and would come to. Every night the thought of her mother not waking up when the cold water hit her, darkened her soul. Lola and her mother had a strong bond. Teri, when she wasn't high, was the most caring, fun-loving person. It was only after drugs entered her life that it seemed like the bond with her daughter began to slip out. As the water bounced against Teri's face, Lola's heart raced and she began to get teary-eyed.

"I told you to use warm water. Shit!" Teri mumbled as she finally began to move. Although Teri was coming out of a nod, she still had a sense of humor. Teri slightly grinned and Lola quickly turned off the water.

"You scared me, mommy." Lola said as she got in the tub and hugged Teri tightly. Lola loved her mother dearly and although she was young she understood the magnitude of her mother's addiction. Lola prayed every night that her mother would get off the drug that the streets called heroin. However, she knew that every time Bunkie Green walked through the door, the drug did also.

Bunkie Green was a well-known dope dealer throughout the city and he was well respected. Teri was his side piece and Lola was a result of their lust rather than love. Bunkie had a wife and kids on the other side of town, but frequently visited Lola and Teri. He actually gave Teri the habit of doing heroin. It was funny because, he didn't care about Teri but he adored his daughter. Lola was his everything and he would come in once a week and shower her with gifts. The bad part about it was, he would shower Teri with product. They had an agreement. Bunkie kept her supplied and Teri wouldn't tell his wife about their ten year old secret. Bunkie also footed the bills and made sure that they needed for nothing. Lola loved her father, but at the same time she hated him for what he made of her mother; a junkie. Bunkie had so much respect in the streets, but his legacy had been lightly dampened because of his gambling habits. Bunkie was notorious for blowing large sums of money on the crap tables.

Lola dried her mother off with a towel and helped her get out of the tub. Teri was groggy but she was slowly coming to as she leaned on her daughter and made her way to the backroom. Lola made sure that her mother was tucked in, when a knock on the door startled her. She quickly looked out of the window and saw the long black Cadillac parked outside. She knew then that it was her father. She rushed to the door and she opened it. The tall, lean man hovered over her with his charming smile and cool smelling cologne. He had a teddy bear in his hand as he smiled down at Lola.

"Hey babygirl," he said as he bent down and kissed her on her forehead. Lola smiled as she felt her father's lips on her forehead. He handed her the teddy bear and watched as she admired it. He never came empty handed.

"Hey daddy," Lola said. She stepped to the side and let him in, before closing the door behind him.

"Where's your mama?" he asked as he looked around and slid his hands in his pockets.

"She's in the back sleeping." Lola answered as she helped Bunkie with his coat and then plopped down on the couch.

"Good." He said as he walked over to the kitchen cabinets and grabbed the coffee jar that had a false bottom. Lola instantly went under the sink to grab his scale and plastic gloves. She already knew the routine. He was about to cut his dope with lactose and package it up. He would always come at random times of the day to bag and weigh his dope. He was a one man show, so he did everything himself.

Bunkie pulled the bag of dope from inside his coat pocket and placed it on the table. Lola stood by the door entrance and watched as she always did. Lola had watched him so many times, she was sure that she could cut the dope with a hustler's precision.

"Go get daddy his magic powder." He said to Lola, referring to the lactose that the cut his dope with. He told her it was magic powder because it could make one ounce turn into two ounces. Lola smiled and ran to the spot where she kept it for him. It was in a jar under the bathroom sink. Lola's naïve mind was telling her that by helping her father with his drug process, she was somehow bonding with him. Lola returned within seconds, gripping the small medicine jar which she eagerly handed to her father.

Lola watched as her father mixed and bagged up an entire ounce of heroin. Just as he was putting together his last package, Teri emerged from the back room. She was naked and scratching her head. Her hair was all over the place and she smiled as she saw Lola and Bunkie in the kitchen. Bunkie looked at Lola and smiled.

"After this flip, I'm going to take you to Cedar Point. Just me and you, babygirl." Lola smiled and loved the sound of going to an amusement park with her father.

"Can Momma come too?" Lola asked, wishing that Bunkie would show her mother more attention. Then maybe he would stop feeding her the poison that ran through her veins on a nightly basis.

"Hey Bunkie," Teri said as her eyes went straight to the packs that were made up on the table. She was like a kid in the candy store in the midst of the drugs. She couldn't hide her excitement as she swayed back and forth while twiddling with her fingers.

"Hey Teri," he said unenthusiastically. He began to put his packs in a brown paper bag and out of the sight of the thirsty Teri.

"Get me well Bunkie. I'm sick as hell." Teri said as she wrapped her arms around her stomach.

"Teri, I'm not trying to hear that bullshit today. I just left you a tenth last night." Bunkie said as he got up and slid on his coat. Teri rushed over to him and instantly dropped to her knees. She was in pure desperation. "Do not do this Teri," Bunkie said as he shook his head in disgust, "Not in front of the baby."

"I need it so bad. I'm sick!" Teri said as she began to kiss Bunkie's gator shoes. Bunkie quickly snatched his foot back and looked over at Lola who was watching her mother's actions. Lola had tears in her eyes and hated to see her mother begging like she was. Lola shook her head from side to side, hoping that her father would not give her any of the dope. Lola was too young to understand the withdrawal phase of being a junkie. She didn't understand that if Teri didn't get her fix, she would be in excruciating pain that only heroin could subside.

"Get up Teri," Bunkie said as he reached down and stood Teri up by her shoulders. He looked at Lola and it hurt his heart that she was witnessing her mother jonesin' like she was. He quickly looked away, not being able to take the stare of his young daughter. He walked Teri to the back and slipped her a tenth pack.

"Thank you. Thank you!" Teri said as she rushed to the bathroom and locked the door. Bunkie walked back into the front room and toward the door. Lola stood there looking heartbroken. She knew what her mother was doing on the opposite side of the bathroom door and it cut her deep. Bunkie bent down and kissed Lola on the forehead and headed toward the exit. He had a lot of runs to make and wanted to get on the road.

"Love you. I will see you later," he said as he reached the door.

"Can I please go with you daddy?" Lola asked as she put her hands together, begging him. Under normal circumstances, Bunkie would have said no. However, guilt altered his logic and he paused for a minute, just staring at his daughter who stood there teary-eyed. Lola didn't want to hang around and see her mother high and leaning.

"Sure babygirl. Go get your coat." Bunkie said as he smiled and gave in. He took a deep breath and knew that he was being a horrible parent but at that moment he couldn't tell his baby girl no. Lola emerged from the back room with her coat on and a gigantic smile. It would be the first time she ever went somewhere with her father. After all those years, Bunkie didn't realize that he never took her anywhere and it dawned on him at that very moment. Honestly, they were both happy to ride out with each other.

The sound of Rick James and Tina Marie's classic hit, "Fire and Desire", bumped through the speakers as they rode down Interstate 75. Bunkie sung Rick James' part as he playfully held an invisible microphone to his mouth. Lola laughed out loud as her father hit the off-key notes from his favorite song. Lola knew the lyrics word for word because Teri would play the song over and over on nights when she wasn't high on dope. Ironically, the song reminded Teri of Bunkie and it made her feel good every time she heard it. She always hoped that one day Bunkie would be hers.

When Tina Marie's part came on, Lola held up her own microphone and sang. *"I wasn't very, very nice I know . . ."* Lola sang in her best Tina impression. Bunkie smiled from ear to ear as he watched his baby-girl hit the high note and he could see the joy oozing off of her. They were both having a great time together.

Bunkie reached his first stop and he told Lola to stay in the car and he would be right back out. Lola looked around and she saw fiends roaming the dilapidated street as she sat alone on the curb of one of the most drug infested areas in the city. Bunkie left the car running and locked the doors before he jumped out. This was the first of many stops throughout the day as Lola rode shotgun with one of the biggest hustlers in the city. Bunkie would park on the curb and hit a trap spot. Lola noticed that his bag got smaller and smaller with each stop. It was the first of the month and that meant money in the ghetto was in heavy circulation. Every time he came back to the car, he gave the money to Lola to count for him. She would count it carefully and then put it in the glove compartment. Although Lola was young, being the daughter of Bunkie Green made her sharp. She had counted close to ten thousand dollars in that car. On days like this, there was no question that Bunkie was the head Dopeman. He only was under one man who went by the name of Larry J. A longtime friend that had a Miami dope connect. Bunkie got all his dope from Larry J and it was time to go see him again. Bunkie had sold his entire product in a matter of six hours.

"Ten thousand in one day," Bunkie said as he turned the brown paper bag upside down, showing that it was empty. He then looked at Lola. He was smiling from ear to ear and shaking his head in disbelief. "You must be daddy's good luck charm," he said as he rubbed her head. He reached into the glove compartment and peeled off two hundred dollars. "This is your cut baby-girl." He said as he placed the two crispy bills onto her lap.

"I can get used to this!" Lola said as she scooped up the bills and held them in the air as if they were winning lottery tickets. Bunkie slyly turned up the radio and pulled off the block, heading back to Teri's house. He and Lola had a wonderful day to say the least and Lola hadn't been this happy in a very long time. Bunkie jumped back on the expressway heading toward Teri's house. A few minutes into their drive, Bunkie noticed a big billboard on the side of the road which read, Spinners Casino: NEXT EXIT RIGHT. It seemed as though the billboard caught both of their attention at the same time. Bunkie's hand began to itch and the urge to make his ten thousand double, created an insatiable hunger.

Bunkie quickly switched lanes and jumped off on the casino's exit. He just needed ten minutes inside to put five thousand dollars on his favorite number; ten. That would double his money and make his day even better. He looked over at Lola and said, "I got my lucky charm with me today, right?"

"Right!" Lola answered as she looked at the lights coming from the casino that was just down the road. Lola didn't understand nor could she even fathom, the chain events that were about to occur just because Bunkie had his "lucky charm".

Bunkie pulled into the parking ramp and quickly parked his car. Lola noticed the look in his eyes. She knew that look all too well. It was the look of someone addicted. Lola's happiness quickly began to slip away. She had never seen that look in her father's eyes, only in her mother's.

"You can't go in here with me. I just need five minutes babygirl, and then we'll go get some ice cream when I get back." Bunkie said as he reached over her lap and pulled out the stacks of money. Lola nodded her head in agreement and just like that, Bunkie was gone. Lola turned up the radio and listened to the "Fire and Desire" track again.

Three hours had passed and Lola had fallen asleep inside of the car. Bunkie finally returned but his demeanor had totally done a one-eighty. He was tapped out. He had managed to lose every dime in his pocket. He got in the car and looked at his sleeping beauty. It hurt his heart that he would have to wake her up and ask for the money that he had given her.

"Wake up baby," he said as he rubbed her hair away from her face. Lola woke up and looked around, slowly remembering where she was.

"Did you win?" Lola asked as she sat up.

"No, baby, daddy didn't win this time," Bunkie said as he pulled his car out of the lot. He picked up his cell phone and made a call to Larry J. He needed to get some work on credit so that he could bounce back. This was the life of a gambler.

Bunkie pulled up to the quiet suburban area that was the residence of Larry J. Bunkie was good friends with the elderly man that had the keys to the city. They were locked up together years ago and had established a bond that stood strong when both of them got out. Bunkie turned off his engine and thought about dropping Lola off first, but he was itching to get back to the money. He had to go get the weight from Larry J before he changed his mind.

"Come on baby. Daddy has to go in for a minute." He said as he talked and moved faster than he usually did. Lola didn't know it at the time, but he was desperate. They walked up the long walkway that led to the door. Bunkie knocked on the door and moments later a tall, lean, dark skinned woman answered. She wore a black silk robe and a beautiful bright smile as she looked at Bunkie and then down at Lola.

"What do we have here? Look at this beautiful little thing. Come on in baby." The lady said as she gently pinched Lola's cheeks.

"Hey Shawna," Bunkie said as he stepped in along with Lola.

"What you got this baby out this late for?" Shawna said as she threw her arm around Lola and guided her through the house. Lola looked at the red carpet and crushed velvet walls. It seemed like a scene straight out of the movie "Superfly". Marvin Gaye was playing in the background and the lights were dimly lit giving it a relaxed vibe. Larry J was a veteran in the game but he was stuck in the seventies and it showed in his taste.

"She's tough. My babygirl rode shotgun with me today. Ain't that right, babygirl?" Bunkie asked.

"Yeah," Lola replied as they made their way over to the gigantic red sectional. Shawna asked Bunkie and Lola if they wanted drinks and they both declined.

"Well, Larry will be out in a second," she said as she faded into the back of the house. Bunkie nodded and clasped his hands as he patiently waited for his friend.

"It'll be just a minute. We'll be out of here in no time," he assured his daughter. Just as he finished his sentence, Larry came from out the back sporting a robe. The smell of marijuana also entered the room right along with Larry J.

"My nigga," Larry said as he held out his arms and waited for Bunkie to embrace him. Bunkie slapped hands with his friend and hugged him.

"Larry J! What's happening?" Bunkie asked.

"Ain't nothing going on, playa. And who is this wonderful young lady?" Larry asked as he looked at Lola.

"This is my baby Lola. Lola say hello to Mr. Larry," Bunkie coached as he pointed to Larry.

"Hi," Lola simply said.

"Hey sugar." Larry said as he sat down and looked at Bunkie. His smile quickly turned into a cold stare. "How we gon' talk business when you babysitting," Larry J said cutting straight to the point.

"She's good Larry. She's a big girl." Bunkie said with laughter in his voice but Larry didn't find it funny.

"Okay, talk to me. I know it has to be important because shop is closed after six. You know that."

"Well, I've gotten myself in a jam. I need your help." Bunkie said as he rubbed his hands together nervously.

"Don't tell me you were gambling again." Larry J said knowing the answer before he even asked the question. Bunkie responded with a simple head nod, letting Larry know that he had fucked over his money once again. This was becoming a reoccurrence and Larry was appalled. Honestly, if Bunkie would have shaken his gambling problem, he probably would be Larry's partner rather than just a buyer.

"You still owe me from the last batch Bunkie. I can't do it. I just can't." Larry J said as he stood up and held his hands out, palms up.

"Listen, I will pay you back. I just need a couple zips to put back into the streets. It won't take me no time to get you your money."

"I just can't do it potna'. I'm sorry," Larry said as he headed to the back. He called Shawna so she could let them out.

"Larry J. Please! I'm begging you!" Bunkie said, putting all his pride to the side by begging in front of his daughter. He knew that Larry had a safe in the back where he kept all his dope and money and it was nothing for him to spot Bunkie a few ounces to get back right. Larry J was denying Bunkie because of principal, not because he didn't have it to give.

Larry didn't even have the courtesy to respond, he just headed to the back and just before he left the room, he looked at Lola who watched silently as the situation unfolded.

"It was nice meeting you young lady," he said. He then looked at Bunkie who had his hands in a praying position. "Take your daughter home Bunkie. Have some pride about yourself," he said just before he exited and Shawna entered. Shawna came in and walked them to the door. She told them both bye, and Lola and Bunkie walked back to the car. Bunkie was so embarrassed and so ashamed of what just occurred. The fact that his so-called friend had just rejected him deeply hurt his pride. Larry J had just cut Bunkie deep, very deep. Lola had never seen her daddy in this position and she could see the embarrassment in his eyes and demeanor.

They got into the car and Bunkie looked like he was thinking hard about something. Lola asked, "Daddy are you okay?" as she saw him staring into space.

"Yeah yeah, I'm okay baby. Buckle your seatbelt." He instructed her as he started up the car. He reached underneath his seat and grabbed his .45 revolver, slipping it in his inner coat pocket as Lola watched closely. "Stay here. I will be right back," he said just before he kissed her on the forehead and exited the car. Lola watched closely as her father made his way back to the house.

Lola witnessed her father knock on the door and when Shawna answered, he pulled out his gun and forced his way in. Lola's heart began to pound as she couldn't do anything but wait. Her young mind couldn't fathom what was going on, but she would later find out that her father had went in the house and killed both Shawna and Larry. But not before he took all of the drugs and money out of the safe. It was a secret that she had to keep with her until the grave. Bunkie became the man in the streets after Larry's death. No one knew he was behind the homicide, but Lola did.

She watched as they attended his funeral and people gave Bunkie hugs and condolences, not knowing that he was the one who caused the ceremony. At that moment Lola learned the ill side of the drug game. She experienced what the greed and allure of drug money could do to a person's mind. People say money was the root of all evil, but Lola learned at an early age that *not having* money was actually the root of all evil. She also learned what using drugs would do to a person. Teri, her mother, taught her that lesson.

Later that night, when Lola returned home, she found her mother dead from a drug overdose. This crushed Lola and she was forced to move in with her father. But that was short-lived because he ended up getting life in prison. He got caught with fifty bricks of raw heroin only six months after Lola moved in with him.

Bunkie's wife wanted nothing to do with Lola after he had passed away. Consequently, that landed Lola in a foster home until she was eighteen.

Lola went off for school for six years and returned to Columbus with her father's reputation and a hunger to finish what he had started. That's when she met Seven . . . and the rest is history.

Chapter Thirteen

Miami Heat

The sound of ropes slapping the concrete floor erupted through the walls of the building as Ball entered the boxing gym. Head low, hood pulled over his head and hands clasped tightly around the pistol inside his hoodie, he sauntered toward Dame, clenching his jaw the entire time. His eyes scanned the room as he took survey of the ten other feds that filled the room. They were supposed to be undercover as they sparred and trained inside the gym, but Ball was a street nigga with street instincts and his sixth sense was telling him that it was all staged. He wasn't falling for the smoke and mirrors. Dame was prepared and had back up just in case anything went wrong. Ball was clearly outnumbered. Dame had never called a meeting in the daytime to avoid the traffic of business hours. It was always just the two of them so Ball was uncomfortable with the array of men around him. Dame stood in the corner of the room, waiting with arrogant impatience as Ball drew near.

"What's with all the back up?" Ball asked, slightly irritated as he stood firmly in front of Dame.

"Insurance. The deeper you get the harder it gets to remember whose team you're playing for," Dame said sternly as the two men stared at each other hard.

"I know what team I'm on. Not by choice, but I know," Ball replied with contempt, disgusted with himself for what he was doing.

"If that were true you wouldn't need that pistol inside of your sweatshirt now would you?" Dame asked rhetorically indirectly letting Ball know that he was aware that he was armed.

Ball smirked but didn't reply as he shuffled back and forth in his stance.

"What progress are you making?" Dame asked.

"You've heard of the all-star weekend right?" Ball asked.

"Of course," Dame replied anxiously, eager to gain any internal information that Ball could supply.

"We're going down there; me, Seven, and Lola. There's a connect down there that Seven's meeting with. Some big time nigga out of Miami," Ball informed.

"I need a name," Dame said.

"I don't have a name," Ball answered as he pulled on his fitted cap, obviously uncomfortable.

Dame moved in close to Ball and whispered harshly in his ear. "Stop the bullshit. I need names! You know I need names! This entire case is in the details. If Seven is meeting someone to cop in Miami, then that's a connection that we need to know about. I need a name."

"I don't have a fucking name man. Seven ain't stupid. I'm on a need to know basis. As a matter of fact everybody from Lola on down is on a need to know basis with that nigga. He doesn't move sloppy, so I gotta play the game at his pace. If I rush the friendship and try to get him to give me info that he ain't volunteering, I end up dead. The nigga will put two in me without even thinking twice," Ball hissed.

"He wouldn't dare," Dame responded. "He doesn't commit the murders. He just puts in the orders. What makes you think otherwise? Have you seen him com-mit a homicide?" Dame's suspicion was peaked as he stared at Ball suspiciously.

"I don't gotta see it. The nigga built like me and I would make a nigga extinct if I even thought he was fishing around in my pond. You got to let me do this at a slow pace, or not at all," Ball said.

"Don't forget, I'm calling the shots," Dame chal-lenged. "You don't do it and I'll have a 10x10 cell wait-ing with your name on it."

"As long as I'm the one in there, I'll take it at my pace. You need me Dame. You'll never get another nigga this close to Seven and you know it. You asking me to dig for names? Is that pig shit coming out of you?" he in-sulted. "I know how to play it."

Dame's temper flared as his temperature rose at Ball's blatant disrespect.

"Seven is expanding his operation. He's moving from dope to coke so the meeting with this connect is impor-tant. I don't know the when's, where's, or who's . . . all I know is that it's going down in Miami, at All-star weekend and I've been asked to come," Ball continued, putting the bravado to the side and getting back to the task at hand.

Dame nodded his head as he felt a sudden adrena-line rush. He was close to closing the biggest case in his career. He would surely be put on the fast track if he could catch this infamous fish.

"We'll be down there in a room at the Rodeway Inn. We've done operations there before, so every-thing should run smoothly. We don't want to be in the middle of the hustle and bustle. You'll come to us to get wired up before you go to the meeting with the con-nect," Dame said.

"And if I can't get away?" Ball asked.

"You'll think of something. You have to. Because if you go into that meeting without coming to see me first, I'll get the warrant for your immediate arrest," Dame threatened.

Ball walked out of the gym, shaking his head as extreme guilt overwhelmed him. He was doing some snitch shit and taking down one of the most loyal, thorough men he had ever encountered. Under better circumstances, Ball and Seven could have done great business together. But in his current state, the two couldn't co-exist. Ball's livelihood depended on Seven's demise and although Ball was aware that he was pulling some snake shit, he had to look out for his own best interests. As he walked through the gym one of the feds eyed him harshly. Ball grilled the white man and stuck up his middle finger before storming out of the building.

Ball, Lola, and Seven pulled up to Port Columbus International Airport, and waited as the driver of the luxury limousine opened the door. Both men exited first and Lola waited patiently as Ball reached back to help her from the car. Seven smiled and shook his head. "Always a diva," he said.

"No, I'm not a diva baby. Ball just knows how to be a gentleman, unlike somebody I know," she replied as she walked past him and nudged him with her elbow. The driver unloaded their bags and Lola took her Louis Vuitton briefcase, leaving the rest of her four-piece set for the men to get. "I have the reservations. I'll check us in while you guys get the bags," she said.

She walked off, high heels murdering the pavement as her hips hypnotized every man she bypassed.

She had Seven and Ball's full attention as she walked around the people waiting in line to approach the counter.

"Damn," Ball said.

Seven patted his man's back and gripped his shoulder as he spun him back toward the luggage. "She'll be the death of you my nigga trust me," Seven said with a chuckle as he flagged over a bellboy. He pulled out a platinum money clip and peeled off a hundred dollar bill. "Yo, my man. I need these taken inside to the young lady at the counter," Seven said as he pointed to Lola and handed the kid the money.

As Ball walked inside with Seven, it felt as if they were going on a vacation instead of business trip. The friendship with Seven seemed genuine and it ate at Ball's conscience that he was conspiring to tear down the empire that Seven had built from the ground up.

Lola approached them and handed them their first class tickets. "Nobody will be in the first class cabin with us. I bought out the entire section so that we wouldn't be bothered," she said as she lowered the mocha colored Burberry glasses over her eyes. They boarded their flight and sat back as the plane lifted into the beautiful sky. Seven sat beside Ball and Lola took the seat across from them, immediately putting a sleeping mask over her face.

This trip was important for Seven. There was only so much territory he could occupy in Columbus with the dope. He had to move into cocaine distribution if he truly wanted to lock down his region. He had allowed the other hustlers to do their thing with the coke game because it didn't directly stop him from eating, but nowadays crack was where it was at. He was missing out on a lot of money. Seven's business savvy quickly convinced him to transition to something new. He was going to supply whatever the streets demanded and this new connect was world renowned for having the best product. All coke, no cut, straight from the fields of Columbia.

"I know I don't have to tell you, but a lot is riding on this trip," Seven stated.

Ball nodded his head. "It's business first. You're the coach. I'm just playing my position. Whatever you need me to do I'm there," he replied.

"That's why I like you," Seven said as he signaled for the stewardess. "Can we get two vodka and cranberries? And also whatever meal you're serving, you can bring that out now as well."

"Right away sir," the woman answered as she left to tend to Seven's request.

"You've got your head on straight Ball. You're a real nigga and I can respect that. I see you going far in this game. You're smart and you're a leader. I dig how you carry yourself. You remind me a lot of myself," Seven praised.

Seven's conversation was like rubbing salt on an open wound for Ball and he felt like shit as he replied. "Thanks fam."

"A lot of men in your position would be gunning for my spot. They would be moving prematurely and asking for a role that they can't handle. You move slowly. You're patient. Loyal. A lot of niggas don't get it but that's the secret to lasting in this game. It takes loyalty," Seven said as the stewardess delivered their drinks and meals.

Ball and Seven took their drinks, but looked at their food skeptically. "Damn I should have ate at the airport," Ball said with a laugh.

"Don't worry about it. We eating like king's in M.I.A. Just get something on your stomach so I can get you fucked up young boy," Seven said as he downed his drink.

Ball followed his lead and took his glass of liquor to the head, wincing slightly from the bite of the strength. "I thought you said it would be all work and no play."

"Nah, we'll have plenty of time for relaxation after the meeting is over," Seven informed.

"Good, good. I've got a little chick down there that I might get at while I'm in town," Ball said.

Seven lifted his plastic cup and tapped it against Ball's. "You got em' in every city huh?" he joked.

Ball's thoughts drifted briefly to his dead fiancée. He knew it was the farthest thing from the truth, but he nodded his head arrogantly. "It ain't shit. Just a broad I used to fuck with whenever I came to town."

"Ughh, this conversation is boring me," Lola groaned as she pulled up her eye mask and reached over for Ball's drink. She sipped it slowly and handed it back to him, "Nobody wants to talk about your little jump off."

Ball sensed a hint of jealousy in her voice and winked his eye at her as her tight lips curved upward in a smile.

The sun shined in Miami and the wind from the Atlantic Ocean blew the palm trees peacefully as the threesome emerged from the airport.

"The meetings' not until seven o'clock," Seven said as they entered the limo that was waiting curbside for them. "That'll give us some time to clean up."

They made their way to the Palms Hotel and checked into their respective rooms. "Meet me in my room at 6:30. Don't be late," Seven said, speaking directly to Ball. "Lola we'll check in with you after we get back, ma. Enjoy the day, do the spa thing, whatever you want. It's on me."

The three went their separate ways and Ball immediately rushed into his room, locking the door. He put
the deadbolt in place just to ensure that no one could
come into his room. He scoured his room looking for
any sign that it had been bugged and after a half hour
of searching he felt secure. He picked up his cell phone
and sent a text message to Dame.

Just arrived. I'm on my way. What room number?

Minutes later Dame responded . . . *Room 814*

Ball looked at the clock and saw that he had three
hours before he needed to meet Seven. He walked out
onto the balcony and admired the view of the ocean.
The luxury, five-star hotel sat directly in the middle
of South Beach and he couldn't help but think that he
was living the life. This was the type of lifestyle he had
hustled so hard to provide his woman with, until all the
pieces came crashing down. Now that he had finally
attained it, he couldn't help but be disappointed that it
was only temporary.

Ball left the hotel and caught a cab to the inn where
Dame was waiting.

"How did you get away?" Dame asked.

"Just strap me up," Ball replied. Being in Dame's
presence put a bad taste in Ball's mouth. Dame was like
a mirror showing Ball his two faces. He had turned into
the same type of man that he despised; a snitch.

Ball removed his shirt as an agent taped the wire to
his rock hard abs. "You can speak regularly. This wire
is sensitive so it will pick up the slightest sound . . . even
a whisper, so just act natural."

Ball nodded his head as he buttoned up his shirt.
"Let's just get this over with," he mumbled. "Just for
the record, Seven's a good dude."

"Seven's a drug dealer and a murderer," Dame answered matter-of-factly.

"How many people have you shot with your gun?" Ball countered. "I'm sure you've nabbed a few drug dealers too . . . how much of their weight did you leave off of your reports?"

Dame's temple throbbed as he stood toe to toe with Ball, but he didn't respond.

"Exactly! It's all the same," Ball spit before leaving Dame's hotel and heading back to his own.

When he entered the lobby he saw Lola headed his way. Her flawless figure was covered in an Yves Saint Laurent swimsuit that complimented the curves of her body.

"Hey, where you coming from?" she asked.

"I had to clear my head," he lied, unable to look her in the eye.

She put her hand on his face and turned his face to hers as she peered at him.

"Seven likes you. Seven doesn't like anybody. You're in the big leagues now, baby." she said.

He grabbed her hand and kissed her wrist. "I'ma holla at you when we get back," he said, rushing off to calm his nerves. Lola's presence had him nervous and he didn't know if it was because of his own anxiety or because of the sexual tension between them. All he knew was that he needed to get his mind right for what he was about to do.

"Damn whoever this nigga is, he's getting it," Ball said as the limo pulled up a massive estate. He couldn't help but be impressed by the grandness of the Mediterranean inspired mansion. He had thought that Seven was at the top of the game until he stepped foot on the marble walkway outside of the 15,000 square foot home. It was then that he realized, this was a level of the game that he had never encountered. At this level it was no longer a hustle. It was a business and Ball realized he was in over his head. The home was guarded better than a military base as he noticed the armed henchmen positioned strategically in every hidden nook of the mansion's shadow.

"You look nervous. You a'ight?" Seven asked, assuming that Ball was intimidated.

"I'm good fam," he replied, shaking the stars from his eyes as he followed Seven to the front door.

"Yo why didn't you invite Lola to come?" Ball asked curiously.

"Lola is a pretty face, and sometimes a pretty face can distract from hidden intentions. I don't trust her all the way yet. I respect her and I embrace her off the strength of what her father used to do, but she still has some work to put in before I allow her access to something this big," Seven stated.

Ball felt honored that although Seven had known Lola longer, he had chosen him to come. Seven trusted Ball, which would only make the sting of betrayal that much greater when the truth came out. They were stopped by a guard as they entered the home and Ball began to sweat bullets as he realized how much he was risking by walking into the place wired.

Seven held up his arms for the burly man to search him for weapons, but a voice from the second floor foyer put him at ease.

"You can lower your arms Seven. There is a metal detector built into my front door. I know you and your guest aren't strapped," a woman's voice said.

Ball and Seven looked up in awe as the most beautiful woman they had ever seen walked down the steps. Her long, white editor-cut Chanel pants were tailored perfectly, covering just enough of her Zanotti peep toes to still reveal her fresh pedicure. Her brown skin was tanned and glowing as she approached them. She radiated class and a bit of arrogance as she introduced herself.

"I'm Anari. It is nice to meet you Seven. I have heard some very impressive things about you," she said. "You come highly recommended by someone that I trust with my life."

"I have to say that this is unexpected," Seven replied, completely smitten with his new connect. She radiated power and a confidence that he had never encountered. "I was under the impression that I was meeting with a Tony."

She simply gave him a smile and held out her hand. "Let's take this into the dining room gentlemen," she said.

Her walk was filled with authority, but it was also soft and feminine. She was a boss in her own right and everything about her reminded them that they were beneath her and lucky to even be in her presence. She sat in a chair at the head of her long dining room table and motioned for them to have a seat. Ball couldn't help but notice the five men that stood silently around them, one in each corner of the room and one seated directly at the table. His hands began to sweat as he thought about the wire he was wearing.

He was so nervous that he felt his body heat rising as a light sweat broke out on his forehead. Ball could hear each beat of his heart and the rhythm was so loud that it drowned out all conversation. All he heard were the subtle threats that Anari was throwing out. Her status was intimidating. He had thought the connect would be some old man from Mexico; a backyard connect with access to a few bricks. But Seven actually had a plug!

Anari sat back watching both men closely as her slanted eyes took in their every movement. Every gesture, every blink of the eye, and every tap of a foot against her expensive tiled floor; she noticed it all. Her freedom depended upon her ability to weed the snakes out of the grass and to her displeasure she sensed something fishy in the air.

She sat back in her chair and crossed her legs, her foot kicking the 9 mm handgun that she had strapped underneath the table. Seven was speaking, but she was barely listening. Her attention was on Ball who couldn't sit still or meet her with direct eye contact.

"Is everything all right?" she asked her eyebrows creased in suspicion. "You're sweating an awful lot."

Ball's heart stopped as he wiped his forehead and looked directly at Anari for the first time since being in her presence. Seven looked at Ball like he was crazy, knowing that it was out of character for him to be so on edge.

"I'm good . . . I'm sorry about that. I had some bad food on the flight down. Do you mind if I use your bathroom to clean myself up a little bit?" he asked.

Seven eyed Ball as if to say, *fuck is wrong with you?* Seven knew that the slightest little thing could fuck up his dealings with Anari, and Ball was blowing it. He immediately began to second guess his decision to bring him along.

"Are you sure that's all that's wrong?" Anari asked kindly, but with hidden meaning behind her words.

"I'm just a little tore up. That's all. Where's the bathroom?" he asked again. The way that Anari was looking at him made him feel transparent. It was as if she could see through his clothing . . . like she already knew the larceny he had in his heart.

She was silent for a minute straight as she stared at him. The bodyguards in the room were all fingering their waistlines as the tension grew thick. They were ready to fire at any moment and Ball knew that he was on thin ice. Finally she pointed toward the hall, showing him which direction to go. He practically jumped out of his seat as he left the room and rushed inside the bathroom. As soon as he was inside he checked for cameras and the breathed a sigh of relief against the locked door. He fumbled as he unbuttoned his shirt and snatched the wire from his chest.

That fucking bitch is going to dead me in this mu'fucka, he thought, kicking himself for acting so hot. The feds had no fucking clue who they were dealing with. He had a feeling that Anari's reach was way longer than the Federal Bureau, and he wanted no parts in crossing her. He threw the wire in the toilet and flushed it repeatedly to make sure that it had gone down. He stood over the vanity and lowered his head as he breathed deeply to calm himself. *Get it together,* he told himself. He exited the bathroom and as soon as he stepped foot in the hallway he was immediately grabbed up and dragged back into the dining room. Ball bucked against the bodyguard as he stared in bewilderment at Seven and Anari.

"Fuck is this?" he asked.

"You've been vouched for by someone that I trust Seven . . . which means I trust you. Now I'm asking you . . . do you vouch for him?" she asked nodding toward Ball.

Seven stared Ball in the eyes and nodded his head surely. "I'll vouch for him," he said without hesitation.

"He's acting like a fucking cop," Anari spat as if the word cop gave her a bad taste in her mouth.

"Yo, no disrespect, but my people are one hunnid. If he says it's the food, it's the food. He's okay," Seven said.

"For your sake I hope so," she replied in a deadly tone. She walked over to him with the precision of a runway model as she stood directly in front of him. "Open your shirt," she ordered. The other bodyguards in the room had already begun to unroll large sheets of plastic and Ball's life flashed before his eyes.

The goons let him go and Ball snatched his arms free as he stood toe to toe with Anari. He kept her eye contact as he slowly undid the buttons on his shirt. He knew that his life hung in the balance. He had removed the wire just in the nick of time, and as he stood there bare-chested in front of Anari, her mug of distrust never changed. Ball couldn't read her emotions. Her poker face was too strong to break.

She patted his face softly. "A woman in my position can never be too careful," she said unapologetically as she reclaimed her seat at the top of the table. "Let's get back to business."

"That bitch was about to blow both of our brains out!" Seven exclaimed as they both exhaled in relief while riding away from Anari's estate. "Fuck was wrong with you? You almost got us killed!" Seven was so high after establishing his new connect, that he couldn't even be mad at Ball. At the end of the day, everything had worked out in his favor and as they rode away Anari was arranging for a hundred kilos to be delivered to Seven's Ohio warehouse.

"Nigga I told you my stomach was fucked up," Ball said. He had come close to death that night. He was playing with fire and with a woman like Anari involved, the stakes of the game had just risen. "Why you ain't tell me we was meeting with a bitch?"

"That was a surprise to me just like it was to you," Seven said. "Bitch is boss though and we in there, baby! Tonight is a good night. Call Lola and tell her to get ready for the game."

"It's time to play?" Ball asked.

"It's time to celebrate," Seven replied.

Lola walked into the arena, turning heads as she walked by Seven and Ball's side. They sat center court on the sideline as Seven mixed and mingled with the celebrities in attendance, clearly familiar with all of the industry's heavyweights. The entire arena was packed. There wasn't an empty seat in the house as the popular All-Star Game played out before them. Everybody was in attendance. From hustlers to celebrities, everyone had come out to party amongst the elite. Lola fit in perfectly as everyone thought she was a high paid fashion model or video vixen. Ball was amazed by it all. Seven was truly showing him the finer side of things. The players on the court were giving a great show and hustlers courtside placed big money side bets on the outcome of the game. Seven and the most valuable players on his team did it up big, partying the night away as they enjoyed the festivities.

"This is it fam . . . this is the life," Ball said as he nodded his head, impressed by Seven's hood prestige.

"This is the beginning, Ball. After what we established tonight . . . this is just the beginning," Seven replied.

Ball couldn't help but think that it was the beginning of Seven's end, but he pushed his rat status to the side for the night to enjoy the present. In the sea of a thousand faces, one stood out amongst the crowd and it was one that made Ball's rage flare.

Seven immediately took notice. "What's good? You all right?"

"I see an old face. A nigga who thought I wouldn't catch up to him. It's the nigga a few rows back and to the left in the black Detroit hat," Ball described.

Seven didn't move his eyes, but nodded his head for Lola to look back. He didn't want to send off any red flags by ice grilling in the middle of the game. Even if the dude caught Lola looking, he wouldn't think twice about it because of her angelic face.

"Yeah I see him," she confirmed.

"The nigga tried to kill me. I owe his ass a dirt nap, nah mean?" Ball stated.

Seven nodded his head and turned back toward the game. "Enjoy the game. These tickets cost a small fortune. That nigga will be somebody's memory by the end of the night. There's a time and place for everything."

Chapter Fourteen

Remember me?

Ralphie watched as the lady seductively stripped for him. He sat in his plush suite on the top floor of Four Seasons hotel. His big belly hung over his waist, so he couldn't see his erection but he knew it was there. The smooth sounds of contemporary Latin music filled the air as the woman danced seductively to the beat. Ralphie licked his lips as he thought about how he was going to pound her within the next few minutes. He had taken two Viagra pills and was well prepared to have a good time. His crew was on the third floor in the standard rooms with their lady friends, while Ralphie had the whole suite to himself. He had managed to do good for himself in the New York black market. A well-deserved vacation to Miami for the All-Star weekend was nothing short of what he imagined it would be . . . fantastic.

Ralphie turned up the bottle of Hennessy as he began to grab his crotch and rub his shaft through his pants. He looked at the black beauty queen and smiled knowing that if he didn't have money, their union wouldn't be possible. He picked her up outside the sports arena and after a few drinks at a nearby bar, they negotiated a deal for sex.

"Okay, Papi. You ready for me to put this pussy on you?" The woman said as she stripped down to her lace panties and bra. Ralphie couldn't take his eyes off the woman's wide hips and slim waistline. It seemed as if she jumped straight off the pages of a vixen magazine. She grabbed Ralphie by the hand and helped pull his big body off the chair. She sexily swayed her hips, making her booty jiggle with each step she took. The way her assets moved, it seemed as if each cheek had a mind of its own and it wobbled without reason. Ralphie's eyes were glued to her backside as they made their way over to the California king-sized bed. Ralphie sat down on the bed and the woman forcefully pushed him down and straddled him.

"Just lie down and I'll take care of you. But, first thing's first. I need that paper." She said rubbing her fingers and thumb together, giving the classic gesture that meant "pay me".

"Come on. I'll give it to you afterwards," Ralphie said as he grabbed her big juicy butt cheeks and squeezed them, making them spill out of his small hands.

"That wasn't the agreement, Daddy. Come on, just break bread and I will ride you like a stallion." She ensured him as she unbuttoned her bra and released her perky breasts. Her dark brown nipples were at least three shades darker than her actual breasts, and the sight turned Ralphie on full throttle. Ralphie couldn't wait any longer and he swiftly dug into his pocket pulling out a wad of money. He threw it in the air and it rained big faces as the lady basked in the money shower. She smiled and bent over and began to kiss Ralphie's double neck. The woman climbed off of Ralphie and pulled down his pant, revealing his red erect penis. He was much larger down there than what she expected. She began to stroke him with one hand, while massaging his balls with the other. Ralphie threw his head back in pleasure as his eyes began to roll in the back of his head. The woman then grabbed a pillow and pulled the pillow case from it. She ripped the cotton and made a blindfold. Ralphie smiled as he was enjoying her creative kinkiness.

"Can you fuck me in the ass," the woman asked as she smacked her own backside making her butt jiggle and sting.

"Hell yeah, baby. I will do whatever you want me to do," Ralphie responded as he was entering a realm of complete bliss. The woman put the blindfold on Ralphie and bent down to whisper in his ear. "Lemme go get the lube, baby. I want you to hit it good and hard for me," she said seductively. Ralphie waited in complete darkness as he laid there blindfolded.

Seconds passed and the woman had not returned. He was getting anxious. "Come on baby. Let's get this party started." After he didn't get a response, he pulled off his blindfold and what he saw almost gave him a heart attack. He was caught completely off guard as two men stood in front of him with guns in their hands.

"What the fuck?" Ralphie said as he sat up and quickly pulled up his pants. He looked across the room and saw the woman who was just his seductress, shaking her head and putting back on her clothes.

"What took y'all mu'fuckas so long? I had to touch his nasty ass dick," Lola said as she held her hand out not wanting it to touch the rest of her body. The two mean standing in front of him were Ball and Seven. Ralphie had just been caught slipping, and once he saw Ball's face he knew that karma had come back full circle. Ralphie was speechless and he felt like he had an apple in his throat.

"Yo, I got this. It's personal." Ball said as he looked over at Seven.

"Cool. I told you Lola was a beast," Seven said as he looked over at her as she made her way to the bathroom. Lola was what you call a jack of all trades. She was deadly, but also sexy which worked out for them in this situation. Seven had put the plan together right there at the basketball game and with the collaborative effort, they got Ralphie right where they wanted him. He had devised a perfect plan within minutes, and Ball witnessed first-hand why Seven was the man who ran the streets of Columbus. He was a street genius.

With Ralphie's crew a floor away, they would make this a smooth operation. Seven gave Ball a pound and headed to the exit along with Lola, leaving the two men in the room alone.

"Long time no see," Ball said as he pointed his gun directly at Ralphie's chest.

"Man, what the fuck? You know the rules of the game. I just was playing for keeps. That's the streets . . . you rob and get robbed. You know that," Ralphie said trying to find any way to mind-fuck Ball and talk his way out of the situation.

"I lost more than you know." Ball said as a tear began to cascade down his cheek. As he held the gun to Ralphie's head, flashes of him holding the gun and pointing it at Zoey entered his mind.

"Listen Braylon . . ." Ralphie tried to explain as he held both hands out in front of him, shielding himself from the gun.

"My name is Ball!" Ball screamed correcting him before he could get his sentence out. "This one is for Zoey," he said as he squeezed the hollow tips into Ralphie's body. Ralphie's body jerked from side to side as each bullet pierced his skin, sending him on his back. The silencer on the tip of Ball's gun ensured a smooth getaway as he turned and left a bloody mess for the maid to clean up. Although death was dark, it seemed as if a big burden was lifted off of Ball's chest. He made his way to the lobby and out of the hotel as Seven and Lola picked him up in the front. Redemption had been sought. Ball knew what he just did could potentially put him back in the slammer, but in his eyes, it was well worth it. Ball had done two things that night whether he knew it or not. He avenged the death of his beloved Zoey, and he also proved himself to Seven.

Chapter Fifteen

The Yacht Club

Seven rented a yacht on the last day that they were in Miami. He wanted to celebrate his new coke plug and also it was like an initiation for Ball. Ball was officially part of the crew and Seven had gained respect for him after seeing him put his murder game down. In a lot of ways, Ball reminded Seven of himself. They were cruising on the calm waters of the Atlantic Ocean and the sun was just leaving the sky, giving the clouds a purple hue. Exotic women were sprinkled throughout the yacht as Seven and Ball stood on the top deck looking over the water. Seven was a firm believer in paid entertainment when it came to women. Seven never trusted women and always felt that a woman's company was great, but to know that she would be leaving the morning after was priceless.

"Great night to be us," Seven said jokingly as he held up the glass of cognac. Ball also held up his cup and the two gentlemen. They looked down onto the deck where the goons were dancing with some of the escorts who all were beautiful and blessed in the ass department. Bikinis and tans decorated the dance floor and it was a beautiful sight to any straight man. Lola danced with a girl and talked shit as it was obvious she was feeling good off the Ciroc she had been drinking all day. Lola also had on a bikini and her body seemed to over-

shadow any of the beauty queens onboard. Her tattooed body and slight cellulite was flawed but offered
a certain amount of sexiness and realness that perfect
Barbie looking girls couldn't provide.

"Yo, you ever hit that?" Ball asked as both of the
men's eyes were on Lola. Not being able to deny her
thick, eye-catching body.

"Nope. And I never would either."

"Word? You can't tell me that you never thought
about it." Ball stated as he watched her laughing and
joking around with one of the goons.

"Lola is like my sister. She's good people and she
came from the bloodline of a hustlers. She was born
to do this. It's always good to have people around you
who understand the loyalty and hard work it takes to
be successful in distribution," Seven said. Ball listened
closely and admired how Seven ran a street business as
if it was a Fortune 500 company.

"Yo listen, I got a surprise for you." Seven said as he
put his arm around Ball. Ball didn't know where Seven
was taking him, but he would soon find out. They made
their way to the first floor deck and then Seven led him
down to the captain's suite. The captain's suite was
a spacious room under the main floor. They walked
down the miniature stairs and Seven let Ball go down
first so he could see what awaited him. Ball went down
the last step and he was not expecting to see what
Seven had waiting on him. Ball just froze and stood
there speechless, not being able to say a word about the
surprise.

Two Latino women, engaging in oral sex with one
another, lay in the sixty-nine position. The sounds of
slurping filled the air as the girl on top grinded her hips
slowly against the bottom girl's face. Seven patted Ball
on the back and went up the stairs, leaving him alone

with his two freaky lovers. Seven went into his short and pulled out a magnum condom. He grabbed Ball's hand and put the condom in it as he smiled and nodded his head.

"Welcome to the family. Have fun," Seven called out on his way up the stairs. Ball heard the sound of the door being closed and he refocused his attention back on the girls as they continued to please one another.

"Come on, Daddy. Come join us," one of the girls said as she looked at him with her big green eyes.

Ball's rod instantly grew as he realized that he hadn't sex in a very long time. So much had been on his mind and his life had changed so quickly after Zoey's death, sex was the last thing he thought about. The lesbian that was on top climbed off her partner. She then flipped over, and laid on the bed with her thick, tanned legs spread eagle. The girls both began to masturbate with their legs wide open, looking Ball directly in his eyes as they moan in unison and pleasure.

"Oh my God," Ball whispered. He was now at full attention and his shaft was in his hands. He began to stroke it making all of his blood rush to the tip, giving himself a full erection.

"Let me feel you inside of me, papi." One of the girls requested as she got into a doggy-style position and buried her head in the crotch of the other girl. Ball instantly put on the condom that Seven had provided, and he walked up to the big, bubbly behind that was poking out in his direction. Ball rubbed his hand against her wet cat and instantly felt her extreme wetness. She was ready to feel his thick, juicy shaft as she slowly jiggled her butt, enticing Ball even more. She began to eat her lover's box more ferociously, making the girl's leg shake as an orgasm took her to complete bliss. Ball couldn't wait as he slid into the girl from the back, making her body arched upon entrance.

"Ooh," Ball crooned as her warm insides sent a chill up his back. Her juices leaked onto his swinging balls as he slowly grinded her from the back.

"Yes, right there." The girl instructed as her hand slipped down to her clitoris and she began to masturbate while Ball was inside of her. Ball looked ahead to the girl who was on her back getting eaten out, and added heightened stimulation to each one of his strokes. The ripple effect his strokes had on the girl's big butt was eye candy. He watched as he sent what looked like waves through her ass every time he stroked it. He felt a premature orgasm approaching so he slowed down, not wanting the fun to end. He pulled out and climbed onto the bed. He wanted to try the other girl. He laid flat on his back and let the other girl straddle him. She instantly moved her body like a snake riding him like a horse at the Kentucky Derby. She gripped her big breasts tightly as she rode him, putting one in her mouth as she began to lick her own breast.

"Oh, you hitting my spot," the girl said as she looked down at Ball. She reached around and began to play with her other hole, adding to the already great feeling. Ball looked at the Latino that he was inside first and she was watching them while masturbating. Ball couldn't believe his eyes. It felt like he was in the middle of a fantasy, and he was loving every single second of it. As the girl masturbated she closed her eyes and moaned. Ball looked down at her glazed, bald pussy lips and saw her erect clitoris sticking out and hard as ever. She saw that Ball was staring at her and she watched as he licked his lips as if he was hungry for her pie. She then straddled his face and began to slowly rock back and forth on top of him. Ball had two women riding him at the same time and just the thought of it gave him the urge to cum. He couldn't help the sensation and urge to release himself. His pipe got harder and his toes began to curl as he moved his tongue like a snake, while he thrust his pelvis into the girl on his pipe. He was about to explode! Ball felt the release and his body fell limp as the girls continued to ride his face and pipe. Ball removed the girl from his face and the other girl followed suit. He was feeling like a million bucks as he looked at the small ceiling fan on the ceiling. Immediately the girls put on their bikinis and left him lying there alone in the bed. No words, no nagging, and no problem. Ball smiled and whispered, "My nigga!" referring to Seven. "I can definitely get used to this," he said as he enjoyed the benefits of moving with a winning team.

Chapter Sixteen

Down low

Chris Nicks couldn't write the information fast enough as he listened closely to Ball spill his heart out. He carefully listened and took in every single word that came out of Ball's mouth. Nicks studied Ball's gestures and voice pitch as he gave him the candid story of his stint as the state's informant. Nicks was getting the true inside story that the streets yearned to know about. Ball left nothing out as he explained all the details. Ball was giving Nicks the story of his life but on another note, Ball was lifting a huge load off of his chest by telling what really happened. He had been labeled the street's public enemy number one, and his legacy was totally standard. Every day, he had to live with the title of the black Sammy the Bull. In the streets, he was merely the snitch that brought down the black Gotti, which was Seven.

Ball sat there with his glass of cognac as he recounted the night that he considered to be the best of his life. That yacht party was the night that he and Seven established a bond. Ball seemed as if he was in a trance as he stared into space, remembering the good times.

"So he introduced you to his plug in Miami, and in the midst of all that, you caught a body yourself?" Nicks asked, trying to get the facts straight.

"Yeah, that's right. But listen, you can't put that in your article okay?" Ball said as he realized he'd said too much. "Not the murder. You can't write about the murder." He reiterated.

"I understand. I will not publish anything that you don't feel comfortable with."

"So what happened after you guys left Miami?" Nicks asked as he jotted down notes while pacing the floor back and forth as Ball spoke.

"What do you think we did? We went home and got to the money." Ball said proudly as he thought back to that particular time span.

"Could you elaborate?" Nicks asked, never taking his eyes of his pad as he continued to write. Ball leaned back in his chair, closed his eyes, and thought back.

"When we came home, I set the block on fire. Seven had never seen a nigga move like I was moving. Yo' I'm from New York, baby. I'm a born hustler. I was too fast for them slow ass country niggas in Columbus. The block that Seven gave me . . . I had that mu'fuckas doing triple after I put my hands on it. We was getting it," Ball said as he was proud of his ability to turn the black market.

"Yeah, I can remember that shit like yesterday. After we left Miami, that's when Seven and I got real tight. We became like family. All of us did."

Ball watched as his block was in full effect. Cars lined up as his workers served them everything from grams to quarter bricks. Business was good. Ball suggested to Seven that they lower their prices and take over the whole city by building a monopoly. His strategy worked like a charm. Although Seven had *most* of the city on lock, now with Ball on his team, he had the *whole* city. Ball had the block set up like a McDonalds drive thru. The dope was selling like hotcakes. Seven was making a lot of money before Ball came onboard, but now he was making nearly double. Ball had business booming and it quickly moved him up the ranks. Ball always had the ability to get money, he just never had the right plug and market. He was in his element and at times he forgot that he was working with Dame.

Ball took a pull on the weed filled blunt as he sat on the stoop. Younger goons surrounded him as the midday sun beamed down on them all. Ball loved the feeling of power. He had goons around him that would do anything he demanded at a drop of a dime. Seven put him in a position of power and he loved every minute of it.

"Yo, run to the store and grab me a blunt." Ball said as he handed one of the goons a twenty dollar bill. The goon accepted it and stepped off the stoop to run to the store. Just as the boy left for the store, a crème Cadillac Escalade pulled onto the block. All the windows were tinted and all eyes were on the flashy truck. The driver of the truck pulled up to the curb and the back door swung open. Out stepped a slim, light skinned man with green eyes.

"Yo, that's Gay Tony." somebody in the crowd yelled. Everyone, including Ball, stood up to see who this man was rolling up on their set like that. Gay Tony was accompanied by three musclebound guys. All of them were wearing hoodies and their hands were tucked inside the front pockets, obviously strapped.

"What's up?" Ball said as he put his hand on his waistline where his gun rested.

"Whoa, whoa. I come in peace." Tony said as he smiled, showing his straight white teeth. He had wavy, short cut hair and wore flashy silk threads. The first three buttons on his shirt were unbuttoned, exposing his chest hair. As Ball looked closer, he noticed that Tony's eyebrows were arched and his nails were perfectly manicured.

"I need to speak to the man they call Ball," Tony said as he looked at each person in the face.

"Yeah, that's me. What up nigga . . . we got problems?" Ball asked.

"This nigga a homo," he said to one of his goons as Tony approached.

"I see you have a nice little operation going on here," Tony said as he opened his arms and looked around the block.

"Yeah, and what's that got to do with you?" Ball asked as he kept a frown, showing no hints of hospitality.

"I have a problem with the way you doing business. Your dope prices are too cheap. I can't eat with them prices. You're fucking up the market. Yo, fuck the sugarcoating . . . you fucking up my money." Tony said getting more aggressive with each word.

"That sounds like a personal problem, homeboy. Maybe you need to drop your prices." Ball said with a smile on his face.

"Yo, let's handle this like gentlemen. I don't know where you came from. But in this town, that is not how you handle business." Tony said.

"Fuck you and fuck all this negotiating." Ball said as he reached into his waist and his crew followed suit. Guns were drawn and Gay Tony and his three henchmen had guns in their faces. They were overmatched so Tony put his hands up and smiled.

"You got it sweetheart. You got it. I guess I barked up the wrong tree. Please accept my apologies," he said touching his chest as if he were sincerely sorry. "Let's roll," he said to his crew. And just like that, they were back in the truck and eventually off the block.

Ball and his crew laughed as they watched the truck disappear off the block. Ball slapped hands with his goons and they joked on how Ball belittled the gay hustler. One of the goons even imitated the feminine walk of Gay Tony. However, instead of laughing and joking, they should have been loading up their guns for what was about to happen.

The sounds of screeching tires filled the air as three vans sped down the block, back to back. The sliding doors on all the vans were open and gunmen were in each one of them. They held automatic assault rifles and shots erupted. It was like World War III as bullets showered the patrons of the block. It was raining bullets as Ball and his goons were taken completely off guard and all they could do was run for cover. Dopefiends and crackheads were hit by the barrage of bullets as the block began to look like Swiss cheese. Holes were everywhere as Tony's goons sent a stern message: Don't fuck with Gay Tony.

"Ooh, shit. Right there baby," Lola moaned as she gripped the back of young hustler's head. The leather seat was leaned all the way back as she got pleased in the front seat of her Range Rover. Her legs were spread widely and her jeans were wrapped around her left ankle as she threw her head back in pleasure. She pushed his head as deep into her crouch as it could go. Lola moved her hips in circles as the hustler flicked his tongue across her throbbing clitoris. She grinded feverishly against him, soaking up his entire mustache and beard in the process.

"Oh shit . . . oh shit . . . oh shit." Lola whispered as she began to feel the surge of an orgasm. She pinched her nipples, slightly twisting them as she felt herself about to explode into his mouth. "Yesss!" she yelled as her juices squirted from her vagina and onto the young man's face. When she hadn't had sex in a while she always squirted when she had orgasms and these were one of those times. Her body shook agitatedly and her body jerked, making her back arched in pleasure. The hustler came up for air and his face was soaked with Lola's juices. Lola breathed heavily as she closed her eyes, trying to catch her wind. The hustler unzipped his pants, exposing his rock hard pipe. He attempted to get on top of Lola, but she quickly put her hand on his chest.

"What the fuck you think you doing? Lola said as she opened her eyes and sat up. "You already know the drill. I just wanted some head. Nothing more, nothing less." Lola frowned as she put on her panties.

"Damn, ma. You're not going to let me get mine?" he pleaded as he looked at her thick body and plump vagina that seemed to be breathing on its own.

"You got me fucked up. I told you what it was before we even started. You better pump your brakes, home-boy," Lola said as she pushed the unlock button on her truck, signaling him to get out.

"Bitch," he said under his breath as he clenched his jaws and put his pipe back in his pants.

"What did you just call me?" Lola said as she pulled up her jeans and looked at him like he was crazy.

"Nothing," the youngster said as he thought about who she was connected with . . . Seven. He just experienced what women had been enduring for years. He had just been used. Lola was cold and she couldn't care less if he got his nut or not. She just wanted hers.

"I'll holla at you when I need your tongue again," Lola said as she pulled her mirror down and begin to fix her hair. She didn't even give him the respect of looking at him when she spoke. The young hustler mumbled something and stepped out, leaving Lola with a smile and a throbbing clit. She felt good being in control and she wouldn't have it any other way. Just as she began to apply her lip gloss, her cell phone rang. It was Seven. He told her to meet him on Ball's block, informing her that it had just been shot up.

"Okay, I'm on my way," she said as she immediately started up her car and headed over.

Lola, Seven, and Ball sat in the back office of Hazel's. Seven was furious. Veins popped out of Seven's forehead as he paced his office back and forth. Ball was fortunate enough not to get hit by the onslaught of bullets in the melee, but some of his goons weren't so lucky. Over eight people were hit during the shootout. Gay Tony was clearly sending a message to Ball. Seven was irate.

"I can't believe this nigga. We had a mutual agreement. He couldn't have known you were on my team. I can't see that happening." Seven said trying to figure out the angle of Gay Tony.

"It all happened so fast," Ball said as he shook his head in disbelief.

"Yo, I got to make an example out of this nigga. Niggas think shit sweet. I'm going to handle this one myself. A nigga put on a suit and the streets think you've gone soft. That's not the case. Yo, Ball roll with me," Seven said as he slid on his blazer. "Lola, go to the block and make sure everything okay. I'm about to send a message to the streets," Seven said, yelling uncharacteristically. Ball felt good knowing that Seven genuinely had his back. Ball himself was furious about

Gay Tony's actions. He wanted revenge . . . fuck what Dame said about if he murders or witnesses it, the deal was over. All that went out the window in the midst of the heat.

"I know where he lays his head at. Let's load up and get ready for tonight." Seven said as he rubbed his hands together. He would usually just send the goon squad to handle this business, but this time he wanted to go personally. He hadn't been in the field for years, so it was time to show the city who was boss.

Seven and Ball pulled up to a quiet block on the east side of Columbus. Seven shut off the engine and parked down the block from their destination, which was Gay Tony's home. It was a modest sized home with a small yard. The backlights were on and Seven smiled, knowing Tony was home. If he wasn't home, Seven planned on waiting until the got there. Seven and Ball crept up on the side of the house and put their backs against the brick wall, the window was open and they heard movement on the inside. Ball didn't expect Seven to put in work like he was doing and to be quite honest, he was impressed. Seven was a leader that called shots but would get in the battlefield also. That said a lot about his character.

Seven put his finger over his lips, signaling for Ball to remain quiet. He then stood on his tippy toes and took a peek inside. He quietly ducked down and shook his head in disgust.

"What?" Ball whispered as he saw Seven's face frown up. Seven shook his head from side to side and remained silent. Ball then took his turn and peeked in. He looked into the room and two men were in the bed completely naked. It was Tony and another mystery guy. Tony was receiving oral sex from the man and Ball immediately cringed. However, he saw the man who was giving Tony head and his heart skipped a beat. It was Dame. It was the cop that made him an informant. Seven couldn't believe his eyes. He looked closer and was one-hundred percent sure that it was Dame. *Dame is a homo?* He thought as his mind churned rapidly around the situation.

"Oh My God!" he whispered as he quickly ducked down, breathing heavily.

"Yo, let's just go in there and blow both of their heads off," Seven whispered as he gripped his gun tightly. Ball instantly knew that he couldn't do that. For one, Dame was a cop and for two, Ball was in fear that his cover would be blown.

"Let's just wait until they come out. No reason to kill the other dude. He has nothing to do with this," Ball whispered harshly. Seven cut his eye at Ball and wondered was he scared or just being soft. Seven had no mercy but he saw that Ball was hesitant. After a brief moment of silence, Seven nodded his head and agreed with his partner.

"You right. We can just lay low until one of them leaves. Good thinking." Seven admitted. Ball wanted to tell Seven that they should leave, but he couldn't figure a way out of it without looking soft. He took a deep breath and leaned against the house. Now it was a waiting game.

Thirty minutes later, Dame came out of the house. Seven and Ball watched closely as they hid in the bushes. They watched as Dame pulled off and immediately rushed to the front door and knocked. They knew Tony would think that his lover had doubled backed so he would open door without caution. Seven knocked on the door and seconds later it flew open and Tony was on the other side with a silk robe on. Seven instantly put his gun to Tony's head and made him walk backwardly, pushing him back into the house.

"Surprise." Seven said as he walked into the house. Ball was close behind and he closed and locked the door. Gay Tony let out a couple of mumbles that they couldn't make out clearly. He was taken completely off guards as he scurried on the floor. "Get yo' punk ass up." Seven said as he looked down at Tony.

"Seven, what's the problem, baby?" Tony asked as he put both of his hands in front of him, wondering why he was getting ambushed by his colleague.

"You sent your people to wet up my block?" Seven asked through his clenched teeth. He gripped the gun firmly and dug the barrel into Tony's chest.

"We had a truce. I would never do that without speaking to you, fam." Tony pleaded as he frowned up on confusion.

"I want you to meet my man," Seven said as he stepped to the side and revealed Ball. "Now, I'm going to ask your ass one more time and if you lie . . . I'ma fuck up that little fruity ass robe you got on. Did you send niggas on my block?" Seven asked as his trigger finger began to itch.

"Man, listen. I did not know that was your block. This new nigga came out of nowhere hustling wrong my way. You know how the game goes," Tony said trying to make sense of the situation.

"No, I don't know. Everybody knows war isn't good for business. You fucked with my family . . . so now you're fucked." Seven said as he gave Tony a menacing scowl. He raised his gun and pointed it at Tony's head. Ball immediately stepped in.

"Let this mu'fucka breathe. He ain't even worth it," Ball said as he put his hand on Seven's shoulder. Seven stood there with his gun gripped tightly with the homo on the opposite side of the barrel.

"Yeah, you right. Fuck this nigga," Seven said as he smiled and lowered his gun. They turned around to leave and just as they reached the door, Seven turned around and darted to Tony who was still on the ground. He quickly put two bullets through his skull.

"Number one rule; always finish your breakfast," Seven said as he looked down on Tony. Ball looked in shocked and watched as a slow, maroon colored puddle formed around Tony's body, and Seven stood over him with a smoking gun. Seven was a veteran and he knew that if he didn't finish the job, he could potentially pay for it later. He ended the bad situation with Tony and was schooling Ball at the same time. He hoped Ball paid attention to the lesson that was being taught. They left out, both not saying a word to each other.

By the time Seven dropped Ball off to his car, he had totally dismissed what had just happened. He noted the look of concern on Ball's face. Seven knew that separating business and personal life was a skill that came with time.

As Ball got out the car, Seven mentioned that his son had a basketball game that next morning and he invited Ball. Ball nodded his head and closed the door. He had just witnessed a murder and also discovered Dame's down low ways.

"What a day," he whispered to himself as he got in his car and headed home.

It was early Saturday morning and Ball was walking into the elementary gymnasium just after 9:00 A.M. Ball hadn't been up that early in a long time. He scanned the bleachers and saw Seven waving him over to his seat.

The kids ran up and down the court and the sounds of squeaking sneakers filled the air. Ball made his way up the stands and took a seat next to him on the wooden bleachers. Seven was dressed down and it was the first time Ball had seen him without designer slacks and fancy clothes on. Seven wore expensive linens. They were complimented by crispy all-white Gucci boat shoes that added a cherry to the top.

"Glad you could make it," Seven said as he slapped hands with Ball.

"What's up? Told you I was going to come check li'l man out. What's his number?" Ball said as he scanned the court, watching as the third graders ran up and down the floor.

"That's him right there. Number twenty-three." Seven said as he pointed to the shortest guy on the court. Ball looked and saw Li'l Rah playing the point guard position and dribbling the ball up the court.

"Oh okay. I see li'l man," Ball answered as he pulled off his jacket and rubbed his hands together.

"Let's go Rah!" Seven yelled as he focused in on his son. Ball looked over at Seven and looked at how relaxed and well rested he looked. He didn't look like he had just committed a murder just hours before. It was as if Seven forgot it even happened. Ball himself couldn't get any sleep thinking about what happened to Gay Tony.

"You have to separate business from personal," Seven said without even looking at Ball.

"What?" Ball said. It was as if Seven read his mind.

"You have to keep the two separated. Never let what you do in the streets affect you. It's a job. It's the life we chose. The sooner you learn how to never bring your work home, the easier it will get," Seven said as he glanced over at Ball, dropping him gems about life.

"That shit doesn't fuck with you?" Ball asked trying to get a clear view on Seven's mind state.

"It was something that had to be done. Look, we couldn't let that slide. If he tried us once, then he would have eventually tried us again." Seven said as he focused on his son dribbling fancy and going to the basketball rim. He got fouled and missed the shot.

"Finish your breakfast, son," Seven yelled to his son as he stood up in excitement. It was a phrase they used. He always told his son dribbling fancy didn't mean nothing if he couldn't make the shot. So he would tell him 'finish your breakfast', meaning to finish the play. Seven sat down and continued his conversation with Ball.

"Look, that nigga disrespected you. That means he disrespected me. We have to hold each other down. You're like family, and if there's one thing that I don't play about, it's my family," Seven said. Ball looked into Seven's eyes and saw the sincerity. Seven meant what he said when he called Ball family and that's when the guilt began to weigh down on Ball. He knew that he was playing with fire. He had just witnessed a murder and if he told Dame, it would be a guaranteed conviction for Seven. However, Ball couldn't do that to Seven. Especially when Seven killed on his behalf. He just couldn't do it. On top of that, Dame had a sexual relationship with Gay Tony, so that only made the situation thicker. Ball shook his head thinking about how Dame was a down-low brother. *That shit crazy*, he thought to himself.

"Family always comes first," Seven said, emphasizing his point.

"Family comes first," Ball repeated as he smiled and put out his hand and smacked hands with his mentor. In a short time, Seven had taught Ball so much. They were building much more than a friendship, they were building a brotherly bond.

They sat and watched the game and talked about life and their next moves. Ball couldn't help to think about the day when he would have to leave the family and reveal that he was an informant.

"Yo, listen. I need a favor." Seven said as the final buzzer went off.

"Yeah, I got you. What's up?" Ball responded.

"I got this old beef. I need a bitch touched. She lives in Baltimore."

"A female?" Ball asked as he frowned up in confusion.

"Naw, it's not what you think. This isn't an ordinary around the way chick. It's from an old situation I had a few years back. Her name is Millie. She a get-money bitch . . . feel me? I just got word that she got out of jail on an appeal and she could be a potential problem." Seven said with a stern look on his face.

"Word?"

"Word. When my house got sprayed up, I sat back and thought bout all my potential enemies. She was the only one that came to mind. I have to hit her. Even if . . . she is across the country and not even on my radar. I have to," Seven said giving his protégé game to soak up.

"Say no more. You want me to smack her up a li'l or something?" Ball asked.

"I want her whacked. I have to finish my breakfast. I can't leave that situation unresolved, feel me?" Seven said just before he stepped down off the bleachers and hugged his son. Ball was left sitting there to think about what Seven just said. He knew that Seven was testing him at that point. He was going to have to commit murder and if he did that all deals were off with Dame. Ball had to make a choice on which side he was on. If he was to follow through with Seven's orders . . . he would no longer be an informant, but a fugitive.

Chapter Seventeen

A Millie

Ball and Lola pulled up to a quiet suburban area just outside of Baltimore. They had been watching the house for the past hour and they knew someone was inside because of the slew of lights that were on. They were four houses down from Millie's residence and parked on the curb. They had an eight hour drive from Ohio, but it seemed quick because they talked shit all the way there. They discussed politics, life, and bullshit for the entire ride. But there was no time for games now. They had a job to do. Ball was the first to break the silence. "Yo, what's the deal with this bitch in here? Why does Seven want her murked?" Ball asked.

"I don't know. I really don't ask too many questions. If he wants it done. . . . I make it happen. Case closed." Lola said coldly. Ball noticed that Lola had inherited Seven's coldhearted demeanor and was an animal in her own right.

Under Seven's orders, they were to put two holes in Millie's head. "I have to finish my breakfast," Seven said to Ball when referring to knocking off Millie, his old enemy. Although Mille was on the other side of the country and posed no threat, Seven wanted to be safe. Their beef was years ago, but Seven never underestimated anyone. He needed her dead. Ball's reality sunk in. He knew that it was time to show and prove and he almost forgot that he was an informant. He had been hustling and having fun over the past few months and forgot that the state of Ohio was building a case against Seven and his crew. However, when they pulled up the truth was put in his face. Lola pulled out the two chrome .45 pistols that were in the black duffle bag and took a deep breath. She placed one on Ball's lap and asked, "You ready?"

So many thoughts went through Ball's mind as he watched Lola calmly slip on a pair of black gloves. It was as if she had done this a million times before. There wasn't an ounce of fear in her heart. Ball knew that if he went through with the murder, he would no longer be an informant. He would be a fugitive. He weighed his options carefully.

Seven and his crew haven't showed me anything but love. If I tell them the whole truth, will they accept me? Or will he blow my mu' fuckin brains out right then and there? It was crunch time and Ball had to think quickly. He was playing with fire and straddling both sides of the fence at that point.

"Yo, let me go blow this bitch brains out. You stay here," Ball said as he put his plan together in his head.

"Naw, fuck that. I'm going in with you to rock this bitch to sleep," Lola barked back.

"Listen, I need you to watch my back and make sure no one comes in." Ball said as he turned toward Lola. "Trust me," he said as he stared at her with sincerity in his eyes.

"Okay. Make it quick," she said as she leaned her seat back.

Ball stepped out of the car and tucked his gun in his waist. He reached into his pockets and grabbed the set of keys. He quickly dipped behind the back of the house and quietly gained entrance from the back door.

The house was spacious and the only sound was coming from the west side of the house. He could hear the news reporter predicting the weather. He started to slip back out but he was going to finish what he had started. He thought about showing his cards after murdering Millie. He believed Seven would accept him and forgive his deception if he proved that he was on the right side. Fuck it, he thought as he slowly crept through the house with his gun in hand. The news got louder and louder and he saw a woman sitting at the desk reading. He slowly clicked his gun off of safety and crept behind the woman. He raised his gun and looked down at the woman. He noticed that she was reading a Bible. That is when guilt began to sink in.

"Seven sent you for me?" the woman said without even turning around. It was as if she had eyes in the back of her head. Her voice startled Ball, making him grip his gun even tighter.

"You already know who sent me. Let's not make this more difficult than it has to be," Ball said as he swayed back in forth as his nervousness set in.

The woman began to recite the Lord's Prayer and that threw Ball off. He began to think about the consequences of his actions. He was about to commit murder. It wasn't even a matter of his own; instead it was Seven's beef. Ball whispered, "I can't do this," he then grabbed the woman by her arm and turned her around. She stopped praying and frowned as she was tossed like a ragdoll onto her own bed. She was a slim, beautiful woman who looked to be in her late thirties. She had no fear in her eyes and looked at Ball intensely. He pushed her on the bed and put his gun in his waist.

"Look, listen to me and listen to me closely. You have to get the fuck out of here. Leave everything and go! If I ever hear about you coming back here, I will kill you myself."

"Why are you doing this for me?" Millie asked as she looked in confusion not knowing what was going on. She didn't know what to say or do. Was this man playing mind games with her? That's what she asked herself as she tried to peep the logic behind Ball's act of mercy.

"Don't worry about it. Just remember what I said. Leave here for good! Go and do not look back! If you don't, Seven will send his goons for you," Ball said with aggression, trying to make her understand. "Am I understood?" Ball screamed.

Millie just nodded her head in agreement. With that, Ball left the room and out of the back door. He quickly ran full speed to the front where Lola was waiting for him, door already open. He got in the car and she pulled off into the night.

"Did you do it?" Lola asked as she looked over at Ball. He nodded his head yes as he closed his eyes and threw his head onto the headrest. He hoped that what he had just done would not come back and bite him later.

They alternated driving, but both of them realized that they were too tired to drive. They drove a couple of hours back toward Ohio before stopping midway in the Pittsburg area to get a room and get some rest. They found a small motel which was the only one around for the next thirty miles. Lola had slowly been sipping some Hennessy that she grabbed from a corner store once they got outside of Baltimore. She slowly swirled the ice around in her plastic cup as they pulled into the parking lot.

"I guess this is it," Ball said as he pulled into the parking lot. Lola smacked her lips, looking at the grungy spot that they were stopping at. But she knew that it was the only thing close. She shook her head in disappointment and put down her drink. She got out and told Ball she would go get the rooms. Ball watched as Lola got out and he looked at her plump ass that sat perfectly in her black leggings. He had to admit that she had nice assets. Her behind looked like two perfect teardrops and her wide hips only added to the work of art. One would've never known that she was a heavy hitter in the dope game, and just as ruthless as any dope-boy in America. Lola had a way of looking sexy without wearing sexy clothes. Her natural beauty was undeniable. She did what most women couldn't, and that was not relying on tight clothes or make-up for beauty. She had her hair pulled back tightly and her baby hairs rested perfectly around her edges. Ball all of sudden noticed how sexy she was.

"Damn, I wonder if Seven be hitting that?" he asked himself. He realized that he never saw Lola with another male counterpart or companion. "Is she gay?" he asked himself as she disappeared into the office of the motel. He quickly shook off the notion of Lola and thought back to his love Zoey. "I miss you Zo."

Lola came out of the office and got back into the car frowned up. She was noticeably hot.

"What's wrong?" Ball asked.

"These mu'fuckas only have one room left. Fuck!" She said in an irritated tone as she picked up her cup and took a sip.

"Look, you take the room. I will sleep in the car." Ball offered, trying to make the situation better.

"Naw, it's cool. We are just going to have to rough it out. No funny business," Lola said as she cracked a smile.

"I would never," Ball said as he threw his hands up and returned the smile.

***

Ball laid on the couch that was a couple feet away from the motel's bed with his feet crossed. He wore his jeans and a beater as he flicked through the channel before landing on ESPN. The sounds of the shower running relaxed him. Lola had been in the shower for over twenty minutes. The sound of the water running finally stopped and moments later a naked Lola came out. Her small waist and wide hips surprised Ball and he couldn't believe his eyes. He was speechless and his eyes got stuck on her glistening body. Her long wet hair was laid over her shoulder and in a single braid.

"Don't get to happy playboy. Nobody ain't worried about yo' ass. Act like you seen an ass and a set of titties before," Lola said noticing that he was shocked by her nakedness. She was so comfortable with her body that she had no need for a towel. "I sleep naked, so I'm not going to change my program up for you. Believe that." She said calmly as she climbed under the covers and turned her back toward Ball.

Ball didn't know what to say. However, he knew that Lola looked even better naked. Her booty jiggled like it had a mind of its own, and he couldn't shake the image that was left stuck in his head. "Damn," he said to himself as he felt blood begin to rush to his penis. He quickly shook off the notion and continued to watch television.

"Do you ever want to get out of this game?" Lola said as she turned around and looked at Ball.

"What?" Ball asked, not fully understanding her question.

"You know, all of this," she said as she sat up and covered up with the covers. "The drug game, the murder game. . . . the game," she asked.

"Yeah, more than you know," Ball said thinking about the game he was playing with Seven and the authorities.

"I'm getting tired of this. Where's the future in this shit?" She asked rhetorically as she looked up at the ceiling and shook her head. Silence filled the room and Ball asked a question that he had been dying to ask her.

"How did you get like this?" Ball asked as he sat up on the couch.

"Get like what?" Lola asked.

"You know. So hard and so cold. I can see that you have a cold heart, and you just don't give a fuck."

Lola took a deep breath and closed her eyes. "I have to be this way. My mother died right with an needle in her arm. My father was shipped off to prison for life and they left me out for the wolves. Coming from where I come from . . . you have to be strong. You have to be cold. Because at the end of the day, only the strong survive," Lola said as she started to get tears in her eyes. It was so uncharacteristic of her to show her emotions and Ball immediately felt bad for asking. He wanted to know more about her past but didn't want to ask any more questions. It seemed like she had a lot of hidden demons buried deep. She couldn't hide the pain that was in her eyes. It was deep.

"I'm sorry. I didn't know," Ball said as he stood up and walked over to the bed. A single tear fell down Lola's cheek and she quickly wiped it away and turned her face, not wanting to show weakness.

"It's cool," she said as she tried to smile it off. Ball reached over to grab her hand. Squeezing it gently, he smiled at her letting her know that it was all right. His smile made her feel better as she smiled back and squeezed his hand also.

"You know what. You're a good guy. You're going to make some girl happy one day," she said.

Ball nodded as he thought about how he had lost his only true love behind some street beef. His eyes watered up also. Lola knew that he too had secrets buried deep and at that moment, they shared something special. Without saying any words, they both comforted each other. Lola pulled her hand away and looked at the television.

"Oh shit, the Lakers playing tonight?" she asked as she wiped her tears away.

"Uh . . . yeah. But D. Rose and 'em going to smash them," Ball said trying to change the somber mood.

"Put your money where yo' mouth is." Lola said with an ear to ear smile.

"It's a bet. Winner buys breakfast?" Ball said, accepting the challenge.

"Nigga, who you think you talking to . . . a lightweight? Put five stacks on that," she said making the bet more interesting.

"Bet," Ball said as he looked at Lola and realized that she was a man's dream. She was just like one of the fellas but was beautiful as a model. A perfect combination. They sat up all night talking shit and watching the game until they both fell asleep.

It was just after 4:00 A.M. and Ball was sound asleep. That was until the sound of movement woke him up. He opened his eyes and stared at the ceiling fan and watched as it slowly spun around and around. He heard the movement again and he slowly turned his head and saw Lola lying on the bed pleasuring herself. He couldn't believe his eyes. She obviously thought he was asleep and took the opportunity to please herself. Ball listened and watched closely as she swiftly moved her two middle fingers in circular motions over her clitoris. Discreet slurping noises emerged from her direction as her juices created its own soundtrack to her masturbating session. He legs were spread wide and her toes were curled. Her brown nipples were standing straight up and her eyes were closed as she threw her head back in complete pleasure. Ball looked down at her glazed vagina lips and he felt his manhood rising. He didn't want to make any sudden movement because he didn't want the show to stop. He couldn't believe he was witnessing Lola get herself off. It looked so good and tempting. Her thick cheeks were noticeable even though she was on her back. They seemed to pour out the sides of her waist giving Ball the best visual stimulation ever. He slowly moved his hand down toward his growing rod and Lola quickly looked over toward Ball and stopped moving, putting her hand over her mouth. "Oh my goodness," she whispered shamefully. Their eyes met and she was so embarrassed. Ball slowly sat up and licked his lips.

"You don't have to stop, ma." He whispered as he stood up exposing the erection that poked out of his boxer shorts. Lola looked down and couldn't help but to admire his thick black penis. It was thicker than normal and average length. She was impressed by his endowment and it seemed like a black cucumber. She could literally see the head throbbing; slowing swelling and retracting. She involuntarily let out a small gasp. The sight was too much to endure. She wanted him badly. It was like her hand had a mind of its own and it found its way back down to her lovebox and then to the clitoris. "It's okay. Go head ma," Ball whispered as he grabbed his throbbing rod and slowing began to stroke it. He knew that this was the best time to get lucky with Lola while she was wet and horny. He put himself out there and hoped that something would happen. It was about to go down.

Ball climbed onto the bed and watched as Lola closed her eyes and pleased herself, spreading her legs as far as they could go. Her insides were pinks and dripping wet and her other hole throbbed as she took care of the business. Ball couldn't stand waiting anymore. He dipped down and put his face into her wetness licking everything in his tongue's reach. Lola arched her back in pleasure and she moaned his name.

"Ball," she screamed as she began to move her hips in a circular motion, grinding against his face. She continued to rub her clitoris as he licked her insides. Ball grabbed her by her waist and flipped her over along with himself. She was now in the riding position while on his face. "Ooh," she yelled as she began to slowly grind on him while rubbing her breasts. She pinched her nipples and slightly pulled them as Ball grabbed her cheeks and guided her motions. As she felt her orgasm approaching, she rode harder as if his tongue was a pipe. She sped up as she put all her weight down and pressed her vagina so hard against his face that he couldn't breathe. "I'm about to cum. Ooh," she yelled as her eyes began to roll behind her head. Ball quickly pushed her off and stopped her from getting her nut. His dick was rock hard and he was ready to put it down. He grabbed her and threw her on her back. He dove onto her wetness and caused her body to tremble. It was a pleasurable pain and Lola loved every moment of it. Ball slowly began to thrust into her making his long ball sack smack against her other hole. It drove Lola crazy. He went deep and stayed there to make sure she felt it. He slowly rocked back and forth while deep inside of her. They were in perfect harmony and although no words were being said . . . their bodies were communicating. He went fast, slow, hard and gentle. He hit her from every position, but it was not until he hit it doggy-style that she released herself. She climaxed and squirted on his entire pelvic area and also wet the sheets. Ball had never seen anything like it. He kept stroking her as her body shook in pleasure. The sight alone induced his climax and he released himself inside of her. "Aggggh," he yelled as he dug deep and release everything he had inside of her. He flopped over on his back and caught his breath. She also flipped over and panted. Without saying it, they both had just had the best sex of their life. It was pure magic.

Chapter Eighteen

Aspen

It was the weekend that Seven had been telling Ball about for months. A two day retreat in Aspen where Seven annually took all of his crew. This year, Ball would be there to witness what it felt like to be a part of something exclusive and family oriented. Seven rented a private jet and flew the whole Goon Squad along with Lola, to the private ski resort. They were thousands of feet above ground and classic Jay-Z lightly pumped out of the speakers giving the flight a mellow ambience. It was nothing but love on that aircraft.

"I want to make a toast." Seven said as he raised his bottle of champagne and looked around the room at his team. He was doing something that he rarely did and that was smiling.

Ball raised his glass along with everyone else as they focused on Seven who stood up in the spacious G5 luxury jet. "To remain strong we have to be each other's foundation. You guys are my family and I would trade my life for any one of you. Real niggas do real things . . . and I stand by that. This is a toast to the good life!" he said as he slightly held the bottle higher.

"To the good life!" everyone yelled in unison as they all took a swig of their drinks. Ball looked around and smiled, feeling the love in the room; although on the inside his conscious was eating him alive. This was the life he always wanted. Seven finished his drink and headed to the back of the plane, tapping Ball along the way.

"Let's talk in the rear," He said leaning down and whispering in Ball's ear. Ball's heart began to pound as he got up and followed Seven into the small room at the back of the plane. Seven closed the door behind them and told Ball to have a seat. The seats, walls, and ceilings were red velvet and a small glass bar was along the back wall.

"Yo, this is living right here," Ball said trying to conceal the nervousness in his voice.

"Well, it comes with the job," Seven said as he poured two glasses of cognac and grabbed a cigar from the cigar box that was on the bolted down coffee table.

"So, what's up? What's on your mind?" Ball asked as he picked up the glass of cognac and took a sip.

"I see myself in you Ball. This game we in . . . there ain't no retirement plan. So you have to save your bread and get out before someone knocks you out the top position, you understand?"

Ball remained silent and nodded his head as he waited to see what Seven was getting at. He took a sip and let Seven continue.

"I can't stay in this game forever and I need a protégé to give the empire to. I want you to take this shit over. I would tell you the right thing and tell you to save up enough money and get out . . . but I was once young and hungry and if someone told me that, I would have looked at them like they were crazy. So what I'm going to do is show you how to play the game right and establish longevity. Longevity is the key to success . . . remember that."

"That's real shit," Ball said as his heart beat even faster. Not because he was nervous but because he felt that Seven genuinely had love for him.

"I want to show you something. I never let anybody meet my connect, but I am going to introduce you." Seven said as he stood up and walked to the bar. He pushed a red button that was on his counter top. Seconds later, a thirty-two inch television popped out of the countertop.

"This is a satellite monitor. We are about to discuss business with the plug from Miami."

"From the Diamond Cartel?" Ball asked not believing his ears. *This just threw shit in the game,* Ball thought. Ball realized that Seven had so many connects that it was crazy. Ball was understanding the drug game more and more as he ran with Ball. He was connected what the streets called "Black Republicans" also known as the heads of drug distribution. He swallowed the spit in his mouth and it felt like a golf ball just went down his throat. He was now dealing with a whole different breed. He heard stories about how strong the Cartel was. This was hands down the single biggest drug cartel in North America. CNN always mentioned them, but never could report anything about them getting taken down. This was hustling drugs at its finest. Ball was about to have a conference meeting with one of the bosses of all bosses.

"No doubt," Seven answered with a small smirk as he sat down and checked his watch. It was a couple of ticks before midnight and the time that they had arranged for the conference call. Seconds later, the screen popped on and the image of a young, strong featured man appeared on the screen. The man on the screen had a professional, but relaxed look about himself. He had on an unbuttoned Armani tailored shirt, with the sleeves rolled up displaying his inner forearm tattoo. His piercing eyes stared into the screen as he finally spoke up.

"Good evening family," he said smoothly.

"What's up Carter? Right on time . . . as always." Seven said as he slowly nodded his head.

"This must be the youngin' you have been telling me about."

"Yeah, this my man Ball. Ball . . . this is Carter Jones of the Diamond Cartel."

Carter was the first to speak. He rubbed his hands together and grinned. "So you the li'l nigga that move ten bricks a week huh?"

"Yeah, that's in a bad week," Ball said jokingly, causing a smile to form on all of their faces.

"I like this youngin'. Nigga got swag," Carter said as he slowly nodded his head in approval. Almost instantly Carter's smile faded away and he sat back in his leather chair. "You the feds?"

Tension instantly built as Ball grew uneasy. The looks in Carter's eyes were that of a predator stalking its prey; so intense . . . so menacing. His gangster was evident. It seemed as if Ball's heart skipped a beat. It was a moment of silence and Ball clenched his jaws wondering what was going through Carter's mind. *Does he know? This nigga has to know. Why would he ask if he didn't know I was working with the feds?* All of these thoughts went through Ball's head in the matter of seconds. He wanted to say no but he couldn't seem to move his lips to talk. It was as if Carter could see right through him and would know if a lie escaped his mouth. Seven was the person to break the silence.

"This nigga is one hundred percent. I put that on my son's life. He's official," Seven said as he leaned forward matching Carter's stare through the screen. Another moment of silence came and Carter smiled. Like that, all the tension was released out of the room. For the next fifteen minutes they talked sports, politics, and most of all . . . the next shipment.

An hour later the jet was landing and they were finally at their location. The jet doors opened and the stairs lowered to the ground. As they exited the plane Ball saw an all-black stretch limo awaiting them. Seven was the first to descend the steps and he was greeted by an elderly white man, that he would later find out was the man who owned the airstrip. Seven shook the man's hand and discreetly slipped him a brown paper bag. He waved over the crew and they all began to enter the limo. Off to the resort they were going. Seven stood by the door and waited for everyone to enter the limo before he got in. However, he got a phone call on his cell phone and stepped away out of earshot of everyone else. Ball watched closely and he saw the change in Seven's demeanor as he talked on the phone. Seven seemed upset and Ball wondered who he was talking to. Minutes later, Seven finally entered the back of the limo and signaled the driver to take off.

"Everything good?" Ball asked trying to understand what had Seven so upset.

"I don't know. Is it? You tell me, fam." Seven responded coldly as he clenched his jaws tightly, revealing his jawbone muscles. Just as Ball opened his mouth to respond, Seven raised his hand signaling him to stop. He then looked toward the front to the driver and said, "Yo driver! Turn that shit up!" Seven said as an old R&B song lightly pumped out of the speakers. And with that, they pulled off.

Chatter and laughter filled the room as they all sat around a long red oak table having a feast; compliments of the resort's five star chef. Exotic women that Seven had hired from an exclusive service entertained the men as they got drunk and talked shit across the table. It was a great time and everyone was enjoying themselves. Seven didn't say much most of the night. He just sat back and observed, periodically resting his index finger on his temple. Ball wondered what the call Seven got was about, but decided to not think about it. He figured that he was being paranoid and left the notion alone.

Ball noticed that Lola wasn't drinking and she seemed to be spaced out. He knew something was on her mind but he didn't know the specifics. Lola wiped her hands and excused herself from the table. Amongst the chaos, no one noticed, no one except Ball. Ball waited a few moments and quickly followed Lola into the kitchen. When he walked in he saw Lola leaning over the counter with her head down. She was obvious in deep thought.

"You good ma?" Ball asked as he stood a couple feet away from here.

"I'm good playboy," Lola said as she was slightly startled, but quickly shot back the witty response. Ball smiled, loving how she was so sexy but also so gangster at the same time. He never saw anything like it.

"Look if this is about the other night . . ." Ball said, assuming that she was regretting their sexual encounter.

"Nigga, please. I ain't tripping off that. You had some good dick and I was horny. I needed to get off . . . end of story. I'm thinking about some other shit." She said as she looked into Ball eyes and shook her head as if she was disappointed.

"He knows," she whispered.

"What? What did you say?" Ball asked as his heart dropped to his feet. He couldn't believe his ears. Just as he was about to ask her to repeat herself, the kitchen doors flew open and in walked Seven with a glass of cognac in his hand.

"Did I break up something?" Seven asked as he walked over to the refrigerator for more ice. Ball didn't know what to say. He knew that Lola knew that he was undercover and was waiting for her to bust him out. He left his gun in his bags so he knew that he was about to die, noticing Seven had his gun on his hip. But to his surprised, Lola smiled and walked over to Seven.

"No, I was just talking to this nigga about the Southside trap spots. He's been moving through them bricks like water," Lola said as she gave Ball a quick glance as she walked past him.

"I told you when we first met him in Vegas that it was something special about him," Seven said as he dropped the cubes in his cup and leaned back on the counter. Lola walked out of the kitchen, leaving Ball in the kitchen with Seven with his mind spinning. Her words lingered in Ball's mind. *He knows*, that's the only thing Ball could think about as he watched Lola push through the wooden double doors and exit the kitchen. Seven also watch her leave the room and then focused his attention on his protégé.

"Ball, I want to talk to you about a few things," Seven said as he slowly walked toward him. Seven had a blank expression on his face so Ball was unable to read him. Seven grabbed two ski coats from the hook and tossed one over to Ball. Let's take a walk.

"Now? It's midnight and its freezing," Ball said not knowing what Seven was getting to.

"So, you scared of a li'l cold weather? Let's roll," Seven demanded more so than asking.

"Okay, cool. Let me go grab my strap." Ball said wanting to be strapped because Seven had an odd look in his eyes. Seven placed his hand on Ball's shoulder and smiled.

"Nah, its cool. Leave it here. I got mine on me," he said. At that point Ball didn't trust Seven, but he returned the uneasy smile and agreed to leave. They headed out the backdoor and into the night.

As they walked down the resort's path the only sound was the crunching of the snow. They walked in silence and Ball as usual was on edge. He wondered what was going on in Seven's mind. Ball was at a point of no return and honestly wished that he never signed up to be an informant. Ball peeped the area and was looking for placing to run, knowing that Seven was about to pull his gun out and blow his brains out at any minute. The last words he heard from Lola kept lingering in his head. "He knows," she said with a look of grief in her eyes. Ball decided to break the silence and stop playing Seven's mind games.

"What's on your mind," he asked.

"I got a call from a very reliable source. Seems like we have a rat in our circle. I would've never thought that someone that I embraced and took in like family would ever do this to me. It hurts to say the least," Seven said. He stopped dead in his tracks and looked at Ball waiting for an answer. Ball didn't know what to say . . . his cover was blown. It was a moment of silence as the two men just stood there and looked at each other. Seven then reached into his waist and pulled out his .45-caliber pistol. "Back to the house," he ordered as the gun was held firmly in his hand. Ball didn't say anything and led the way back to the house, knowing that he was about to die. However, he wasn't going to run, cry, or beg. He knew that he deserved what was coming to him so he promised that he would go out like a man and not a coward. In his mind, it was the only way to die with some type of respect since he had disrespected himself for the past couple of months.

Chapter Ninteen

Loyalty Over Everything

"Loyalty over everything. That's what it's supposed to be." Seven said as they entered the house. Ball led the way and was afraid to turn around, knowing that Seven would put a bullet straight through his head. "Go in the basement. I want to show you something." Seven said. Speechless, Ball followed his orders and headed to the door that led to the basement. Ball walked down the stairs trying to brace himself for impact. They reached the final stair and Ball noticed the whole goon squad was downstairs waiting on them. Everyone had sad looks on their faces and Ball stopped in his tracks. Seven walked around him and stood in front of him with watery eyes. "I can't believe it." Seven pointed his gun and Ball closed his eyes. Seven continued, "She's a federal agent."

Ball frowned in confusion and opened his eyes. He couldn't believe what he just heard. He saw Seven flip the gun around, giving him the weapon.

"You have to do it. None of us can," Seven said as he shook his head and stepped to the side. Ball looked past him and the members of the goon squad parted, revealing what was behind them. It was Lola. She was tied to a chair with duct tape over her mouth.

"What?" he said as he didn't understand what was going on. He saw Lola sitting there bound to a chair with tears streaming down her face. "What the fuck is this?" he asked.

"Lola. She is a federal agent. She's been working with the feds since the beginning," Seven said as one of the goons passed him an envelope. Seven then handed the envelope to Ball. Ball slowly grabbed and opened it. Ball took out the pictures and saw a young Lola in a photo wearing a police uniform. He flipped through the pictures and saw another one with her receiving a certificate after completing the police academy. He couldn't believe his eyes. Lola was a cop all along.

"I can't do it. You have to. You have to rock her to sleep," Seven said as a single tear slid down his cheek. Ball looked at everyone in the room and they were crushed. Their leader was a snitch and none of them could muster up the nerve to kill her. They assumed since Ball was the newest member that he should be the one to pull the trigger. Everyone else in the room had been with Lola for over three years and it was too painful to stomach. Ball just stood there with the gun in his hand and everyone began to leave the basement shaking their head in shame. They knew that it was mandatory that she had to die. Seven was the last to go. He walked over to Lola and kissed her on the forehead. He couldn't even look at her. "We were supposed to be family and this is how you repay me. Well now, I'ma send you back to the government in a pine box," he said, getting angrier with every word that spilled out of his mouth. Seven slowly turned and looked back at Ball. Seven quickly turned cold and didn't have any regards for Lola's life. She went against the grain and now it was time to pay for her betrayal. Ball clenched his jaws knowing that if he didn't kill Lola, Seven's suspicions would instantly go toward him. It was time to show and prove and he had to do it. Seven stepped to the side, giving Ball a clear path to Lola. Ball raised his gun and walked toward Lola. Lola stared into Balls eyes and there was no fear there. She was willing to take it like a G, and get rocked to sleep forever. Ball knew that it could have easily been him in that chair. The only difference was that he hadn't gotten his cover blown yet. How could Ball kill a woman that he had just made love to? He was torn but it was as if he could literally feel Seven breathing on the back of his neck. He knew that Dame had explained to him that he was exempt from everything except murder...but at that point he was in too deep. He had to pull the trigger or potentially lose his own life. Ball mouthed, "I'm sorry," to Lola and put the gun to her head. Lola didn't flinch. She slowly nodded her head and smiled with her eyes. It was as if she was saying, *I understand what you have to do.* Ball closed his eyes and . . .

"Hold up! I can't watch this shit. Get this over with and put her in the trunk," Seven said coldly as he exited the basement. Seven was in his element and didn't give a fuck. Ball watched as he climbed the stairs and disappeared into darkness. Ball quickly focused his attention back on Lola and dropped to his knees. He swiftly ripped the duct tape from her mouth and she gasped for air.

"Listen, we don't have a lot of time. I want you to run up these stairs and out the back door. There is a path to your left when you get out of here. Go that way and run like hell. I'm going to shoot at you, but I promise I won't hit you. I just want you to run like hell and don't look back, okay?" Ball whispered as he frantically untied her from the chair.

"Get out before he finds out about you too," Lola said as tears streamed down her eyes. She knew all along. It all began to make sense to Ball. It wasn't a mistake that Lola booked the fight tickets that caused the initial meeting with them. She was working all along. But why? How could a real bitch like Lola be a federal agent? She was one of the most real people Ball had ever met: male or female. She was a gangster to the core and he couldn't believe what was unfolding. He had to ask her.

"Why? Why did you get into this? Your father was a hustler . . . and you became a cop?" Ball asked in a whisper trying to make sense of the crazy situation.

"The truth is . . ." Lola said as the tears flowed freely. "I hated my father. Do you know why my mother got killed?" she broke down once again, burying her face in her hands. "My mother died off of a pack my father gave her. Right in front of me! Do you know what that does to a little girl's mind? Huh? My father went to jail, leaving me to fend for myself and enter the system. I hated him for that. So I promised that I would destroy and seek revenge on behalf of my mother. That's when I joined the police force. I hate drug dealers. Drug dealers tore my family apart." Lola confessed as she broke down in Ball's arms. Ball could feel her pain and was at a loss for words. Not knowing what to say to console the heartbroken woman. He knew that they did not have much time so he grabbed her by her shoulder and looked into her eyes.

"Look, you have to go. You have to run and never look back," Ball said as he looked at Lola. For a split second she began to look like Zoey. He was bugging out. He stood up and whispered to her. "Go!'. And with that she took off up the stairs and out of the door. He waited for a few second to let her get a head start and ran behind her screaming.

"Come here bitch!" He yelled with the gun in-hand. He rushed out and began to fire shots in the air as he saw Lola disappear into the night. Seven and the crew came running out moments later and Ball began to put on an act by grabbing his crotch area.

"What the fuck happened?" Seven asked as he looked around in complete confusion.

"She got away!" Ball screamed as he bent over, faking an injury.

"How? She was tied up. Fuck!" Seven screamed, which was something that he rarely did.

"I know, I know. That's my fault. I untied her. I couldn't shoot her while she was tied up. I started feeling guilty. I just couldn't do it to her fam." Ball explained.

"Damn!" Seven said as he put both hands on his hips and shook his head in disbelief. "Load up fellas. It's time to go. This place will be crawling with feds in no time," Seven said before he headed back into the house. Ball looked into the darkness and took a deep breath. He knew that his time was running short. Whoever notified Seven about Lola would eventually bring Ball's situation to light. Ball knew that he wouldn't be as lucky as Lola. Seven was ready to kill Lola after years of friendship. He didn't know then, but that would be the last time he would ever see Lola Banks. Seven knew that his time was running out and he was going to hand over the empire and play the back. Ball was to be the next Dopeman. He was about to put him on to his plug, young Carter of the Diamond Cartel. The supposed drop-off was a week ahead and Seven vowed that it would be his last shipment. He was done.

The eighteen-foot speedboat zoomed across the top of the ocean's water, hitting each wave at almost eighty miles per hour. Seven smiled while a cigar hung out the left side of his mouth and the sun beamed down on his skin. He looked over and saw the other speedboat was neck to neck with him while his right hand man steered the watercraft. Ordinary boatmen wouldn't dare push an $80,000 luxury watercraft to the max; but they weren't ordinary boaters. . . . they were street millionaires that just so happen to be in boats.

An all-white linen shirt hung on Seven's shoulders perfectly, and he left the buttons unfastened to allow the wind to blow through the expensive fabric while displaying his slight gut. He glanced over at Ball, who was driving the other boat, and laughed aloud as he knew that he had won the race. Seven slowed down after he passed the marker and threw both of his hands up in victory. As the other boat approached, Seven looked at Ball and smiled.

"I want my money all in ones," Seven teased as they had just bet $20,000 on the thirty-second race.

"It's nothing," Ball spat back with a smile as he tossed his anchor over board and put the engine an idle. Seven did the same and put out his cigar as he looked down at his watch and saw they were right on time.

"Packages should be here any minute now," Seven whispered under his breath as he scanned over the massive ocean while he put his hand over his brow, blocking the beaming sun rays. Just as expected, a single engine jet came across the skies, leaving a trail of white smoke as the aircraft zoomed through the clouds. Ball looked in the sky and watched as duct taped packages fell from the jet and landed in the water only a few yards away from them. Seven immediately grew a grin on his face and began to think about the money he would get when he turned the powder substance that was in the packages into green bills. Seven looked over at Ball and nodded his head while giving him a smile as if he was saying "Time to get to the money," and Ball returned the smile as he rubbed his hands together.

"Yo, remember this spot . . . the drop-off is always made on the fifteenth marker," Seven instructed Ball as he pointed to the ocean marker. Ball made a mental note so he would remember where to pick up the dope next time around. Seven signaled Ball to hop over in his boat and Ball quickly did just that. Seven, while the boat was idle, guided it to the spot where the packages were dropped.

"Help me out," Seven said as he grabbed a long steel pole with a net on the end of it and began retrieving the dope from the water. Ball helped him load the over-sized duffle bags onto the boat, both of them containing fifty kilos each. They both loaded it onto the boat and a patrol boat was approaching them fast.

"Ah shit . . . we got company," Ball said as he grew uneasy. He noticed a boat approaching them, which contained three uniformed men. A huge U.S. Coast Guard logo resided on the side of their speedboat and the sight alone made Ball's heart skip a beat.

"Relax. Just be calm," Seven instructed as he continued to load the bags onto the boat. "Good evening gentlemen," Seven said as shook his hands dry and rolled up his sleeves. Ball's heart began to beat rapidly as he looked at the badges on the guards that occupied the boat.

"What's going on here?" the man who seemed to be in charge asked.

"Not much. My friend and I are just enjoying the beautiful ocean," Seven said with a smirk on his face.

"Oh, I see," the guard responded.

Seven reached into his glove compartment, pulled out a brown paper bag, and tossed it over to the boat where the guards were.

"Same as always," Seven said as looked into the eyes of the guard. "And smile . . . y'all making my man nervous over here," he added. Everyone, except Ball, burst into laughter as they saw the beads of sweat forming on Ball's forehead. Ball broke down and released a smile too, sensing that everything was all good.

The guard slipped the bag into his inner vest and pulled off just as quickly as he pulled up.

"It's like that, huh?" Ball asked as he couldn't believe that Seven had the police on his payroll. Seven slowly nodded his head in agreement as he pulled his cigar from his top pocket and lit it, blessing the clear air with Cuban cigar smoke.

"You trust that he won't turn on you?" Ball asked trying to understand the angles of the game.

"It's not that I trust him . . . I trust greed. I trust that the money that I'm giving him every month keeps him loyal to me. Always trust greed. . . . It will never let you down," Seven explained as he began to pull the anchor out of the water. Ball soaked up the game Seven was giving him, and he admired the way Seven looked at the game as if it was chess. . . . Every move was strategic and well thought out.

"This is my last flip and I'm done with the game for good," Seven said as he sat in the driver's chair. He took a deep breath and stared into the ocean, obviously in deep thought. Seven grew a somber look on his face as new thoughts emerged in his mind. "I have to do it for Li'l Rah," Seven said.

"How is he holding up?" Ball asked, knowing that he was suffering from leukemia.

"Not so good . . . The doctor said he has about a year left to live," Seven continued as he turned his head away from Ball, not wanting him to see the hurt in his eyes.

"Damn," Ball said under his breath as his heart dropped from of the horrible news.

"That's why I'm about to flip this last shipment and hang it up for good. I'm leaving everything to you. I'm done with this game," Seven said as he looked into the eyes of his protégé. Seven had a lot of love for Ball and in many ways he reminded him of himself. "I'm going to move to Florida with my son and make his last year the best year of his life. We'll go to Disney World every day, and we'll live life to the fullest. We are going to fight this battle head on and hope for the best."

"That sounds like a plan," Ball said not believing his ears. *He's about to give his whole empire to me?* Ball thought as he looked at Seven.

"It's all yours," Seven said as if he could hear Ball's thoughts.

"Listen man, just go. . . . Leave this game alone now. Leave these bags with me and go the other way. You and Li'l Rah should just go to Florida today."

"What?" Seven asked, not understanding Ball's logic.

"You have enough to live so why take a risk and try to make extra money?" Ball asked really wanting for Seven to leave for Florida at that moment. Ball had a bad gut feeling and just wanted Seven to go far away and never look back. Ball felt that the dope game would be better in his hands rather than in Seven's. He contemplated skipping out on the feds and becoming the drug boss that Seven had been preparing him to become.

"One last time," Seven said with confidence. Seven's eyes were piercing and he was determined to follow through with his plans. He had already had his mind made up.

Ball started to contest Seven, but he decided to hold his tongue. He understood that once a man had made up his mind, it would be hard to convince him to do otherwise. Ball jumped back over to his boat and started up his engine. Seven did the same, but just before he pulled off so they could head back to shore and flood the streets with raw heroin. . . . He looked over at Ball.

"Yo!" Seven yelled over.

"I love you fam," Seven said meaning every word. Ball paused and let the words sink in. He had never heard another man tell him that they loved him before. He looked into Seven's eyes and knew that the words were sincere and genuine. Seven was a real nigga and he wanted to let his protégé know that he had love for him.

"Love you too, big homie," Ball replied. Seven slowly nodded his head and quickly pushed the throttle making his boat's front end rise up.

"Double or nothing!" he yelled just before he sped away. Ball burst into laughter and quickly kicked his boat in gear, ready to race.

Minutes later they were docking their boats and ready to unload the bags into Seven's Range Rover which waited at the other side of the pier. Seven had a duffle bag over his shoulder and so did Ball. As they reached the end of the pier, Seven felt strange and stopped in his tracks. He then noticed a helicopter fly over his head and he stared at it. It seemed like everything was unfolding in slow motion. Federal agents came from every way with their guns drawn. Some were even hopping out of the water with automatic assault rifles.

"Freeze, put your motherfucking hands up," one yelled as they quickly approached. Seven smiled as he dropped the bag and put his hands up.

"Don't say anything Ball! I will have us out in the morning," Seven yelled with a small grin on his face. Ball dropped his bag and put up his hands as the feds rushed them. Ball dropped his head and knew that they would not be getting out in the morning; at least Seven wouldn't be.

Chapter Twenty

Untouchable

A custom made Gucci suit hung on the shoulders of the street's king, Seven. He sat in the courtroom with a smile on his face as he fingers intertwined with each other. He sat with posture and strength as CNN cameras were all around giving up to the minute correspondence. He looked back at Rah, who was there with his social worker, and smiled while mouthing "I love you" to him. Seven didn't mind sitting in jail or even fighting with the feds for his freedom. He was built for situations like the one that was placed upon him. Yet, the one thing that hurt him to his heart was being separated from his li'l man. That is what hurt the most in Seven's world. Li'l Rah was his backbone and although Rah was a little boy, Seven needed him to survive. Seeing Rah sitting next to a social worker and not with him, made Seven want to drop a tear. He remained strong and smiled as Rah had tears in his eyes, seeing through his father's phony smile. He knew that his father was fighting back tears and it hurt him to see his hero like that. Seven winked his eye and focused back on the district attorney who was trying his best to paint Seven as a menace to society and notorious drug kingpin.

***

Seven sat before the jury and next to his seven-figure attorney. The trial had begun and it was the eighth day. The district attorney was slated to bring his informant to the stand and Seven wondered who it could be. The truth came out about Lola, but she had fled and the feds couldn't locate her. Lola decided that she couldn't testify, so she disappeared and dropped off the face of the earth. This steamed the feds and all of their hopes and aspirations on locking Seven up, rested at the hands of the state's informant, which was Braylon.

In Seven's eyes, his odds of getting acquitted were looking good because they had no concrete evidence against him on drug trafficking charges. Little did he know, Braylon "Ball" Kennedy was about to take the stand and testify against him. Seven had been in the county jail for six months and was oblivious to the fact that Ball was an informant.

"I would like to call my next witness. I am about to present an informant who infiltrated Seven's organization. He ate, slept, and ran with Seven. All the while gaining his trust and witnessing him break the law by bringing dope into our community. Please bring in the witness," the prosecutor said as he looked at the double doors at the back of the courtroom. The courtroom was in complete silence. You could literally hear a pin drop as all eyes went to the backdoor. Seven's heart dropped as he took in the news. He had just got delivered a powerful blow that made butterflies form in the pit of his stomach. When the doors flew open and he saw Ball walk in. . . . he dropped his head. He knew he was done. Ball was his right hand man. Seven considered Ball his family and seeing Ball walk in confused him.

"I can't believe this," Seven mumbled as he shook his head in disappointment.

Seven knew that with Ball's testimony it was an inevitable life sentence. The game was now over. Seven stared at Ball as he walked up the aisle. Ball never looked in Seven's direction. But he did get a glance of li'l Rah who was in the audience looking at the man who would bring down his father. Ball would never forget the look at the little boy's face as he made his way to the stand. Ball walked pass his former mentor and took the stand.

"Do you swear to tell the truth, the whole truth, and nothing but the truth?" the bailiff asked as Ball stood before him with his left hand on the Bible, right hand in the air.

"Yes I do," Ball said as he sat down in the chair before the courtroom. The prosecutor got straight to the point as he suavely stood up and buttoned the bottom two buttons on his blazer.

"Can you state your name for the courtroom, please?" The prosecutor asked as he slowly paced the floor with one of his hands in his pocket.

"My name is Braylon Kennedy." Ball said clear and loudly.

"What did you go by in the streets?"

"Ball. They called me Ball."

"Do you know the defendant sitting on the left side of the courtroom?" the prosecutor asked as he turned and faced Seven.

"Yes, I do." Ball said as he looked at Seven who was staring a hole directly through him while being tight-lipped. Seven was heartbroken. He knew that he would never be able to raise his sick son and would be going away for a long time. He then began to think about how Ball had shown nothing but loyalty over the past year. He couldn't believe that he was working with the feds.

"You're not a cop," Seven mouthed as he shook his head in denial. He looked Ball directly in the eye. Ball quickly looked away as he understood every word that came out of Seven's mouth.

"Can you explain your affiliation with the defendant," the prosecutor asked.

"I ran with him over the past year. That was my man," Ball answered honestly.

"Can you explain to us the extent of his drug operation?" the prosecutor asked as he grew a small smirk on his face and looked back at Seven. He knew that he was about to put the nail in the coffin with Ball's next words.

"No I can't," Ball said as he sat up straight with posture.

"What?" the prosecutor said as he quickly looked at Ball with a concerned expression. He could not believe his own ears.

"I can't tell you about a drug operation because I did not witness that man sell any drugs. To my knowledge he is a bar owner and great father," Ball said eliminating the grin that the prosecutor had worn just seconds before.

"What the hell are you doing!" the prosecutor yelled as he couldn't contain himself. Ball was destroying the case that they had built. Dame also sat in the audience and stormed out once he heard Ball's comment. Dame was furious. He couldn't wait until Ball got off the stand because he was going straight to prison.

"You heard me. I don't know shit about selling any drugs. I never witnessed or had any knowledge of that. Any more questions?" Ball asked sarcastically.

"This is ridiculous." The prosecutor yelled as he went over to the bench, requesting a mistrial. But the judge wasn't having it. The courtroom had grown into pure pandemonium. Everyone in the courtroom felt a type of way. Some clapped in victory others sighed in defeat. It was crazy. The judge banged his gavel to restore order and then looked over to Seven's attorney.

"Would you like to cross examine?" The judge asked.

"No thank you," Seven's attorney answered as he closed his notebook. The judge dismissed Ball from the stand. Ball stepped off and headed to the rear of the courtroom when Dame was waiting with his arms crossed, visibly irate. Ball looked at Seven, who gave him a cold stare that symbolized nothing but hate and animosity. If looks could kill, Ball would have been circled in chalk right then and there in the courtroom. Although Ball didn't snitch, Seven still felt betrayed. Ball dropped his head and walked to Dame. Ball noticed all of Seven's goons giving him gestures such as pulling trigger, slicing of the neck, and ice grills. They wanted to dead him right there but they knew that they couldn't do anything at that current moment. Ball just dropped his head and proceeded to the rear.

"You're going to prison for life you son of a bitch," Dame whispered harshly in Ball's ear as he grabbed him by the arm and forcefully put hands cuffs on him. Dame pulled him out of the courtroom ready to deliver him straight to a cell.

When Ball and Dame made it into the hallway, Dame exploded. He gave Ball a shot to the mid-section folding him up. "You made the biggest mistake of your life mu'fucka," Dame spat. Ball rose up and oddly he was smiling.

"What the fuck you smiling about?" Dame asked as the grin enraged him even more.

"Because I'm not going back to jail. You are going to let me go and honor your side of the agreement," Ball said confidently.

"Like hell I am," Dame replied as he stepped in Ball's face.

"Yes you are. I know you're little secret . . . faggot." Ball said as he maintained his smile. Dame's heart dropped and he looked like he had just seen a ghost.

"What the fuck you mean? You got me fucked up. Ain't nothing gay about me, mu'fucka," Dame denied as he swallowed what seemed to be a golf ball in his throat.

"I have you on tape with your li'l boyfriend. Does Gay Tony ring any bells, huh? How would your wife and four kids feel about you being homo. Yo . . . what's that? The cat got your tongue?" Ball lied as he dipped his head as if he was waiting on an answer from Dame. Dame was speechless. The idea of his family or community knowing that he was a down low brother scared him shitless. He began to think about his fellow police officers, church members, and family. Growing up in a homophobic community had him jaded and he would protect his secret at all cost.

"I . . . I," Dame stuttered. Ball extended his arms and Dame had no choice but to release him. Dame would have to pull some strings to release Ball but it was something that he had to do. He was fucked.

"We, the jury find the defendant. . . . not guilty." The petite Caucasian lady said as she looked at the note-card that she held in front of her face. The courtroom erupted and Seven's goons, along with Rah rejoiced. Seven shook his lawyers hand and looked at his son smiling. He had just beaten the system. This Dopeman was literally untouchable.

Chapter Twenty-one

Can I live

It was the evening of the trial and Seven celebrated his acquittal at Hazel's. All of his crew was in attendance and so was Li'l Rah. A live band played while everyone enjoyed drinks and shit-talking. One of Seven's goons hired an escort service to provide beautiful girls with skimpy bunny outfits to serve the drinks, just to add a cherry on top. It was to be a night of good times and celebration. As a smooth rendition of one of Lauryn Hill's old hits was being played, Seven smiled in the middle of the party and grabbed his son. He kissed him on the forehead and told him that he loved him. He was determined to take his son to Florida and move away from the madness. The party was a celebration of his acquittal, but in Seven's mind it was also a retirement party for him. He couldn't be happier. He looked over and saw one of his goons put Li'l Rah on the table and Rah danced and had fun with the fellas. "I love my family," Seven thought as he smiled while looking at his son. For some strange reason, he wished Lola was there to share the moment with him. In the bottom of his heart, he knew if it came down to it Lola wouldn't have had testified against him. It was just a gut-feeling that he had. The mood changed when the band began to play Jay-Z's instrumental of "Can I Live" and the place went bananas. Everyone waved their hands from side to side, and the song felt fitting to their gangster way of life and triumphant victory. That's exactly what Seven wanted to ask the prosecutor . . . *Can I live?* He wanted to celebrate his night with one of his hand-rolled Cuban cigars that he kept in his office. He put his son down and headed to his office, getting pats on the back all the way to the door.

Seven grabbed a bottle of champagne from one of the bunnies' ice buckets and went into his office. He walked in and flicked on the lights. He jumped when he saw a man sitting at his chair waiting for him. It was Ball. Ball slowly stood up and both of the men stared at each other, neither one of them muttering a word. Ball knew that it was dangerous for him to come back to Hazel's, but for the past year it was all that he knew. Seven was his family, and honestly he was the only thing Ball had left.

As the men stared at each other the tension grew in the room. It was so thick that you could cut it with a knife. Ball knew that if Seven pulled out a gun and shot him in the middle of the forehead, he would be justified. Ball just wanted his old life back. For some reason, he believed that Seven would let him back in the crew to do what he did best and that was hustle. Seven smiled, breaking the tension and held out his arms. "I knew you weren't going to turn on me," Seven said as he stepped toward Ball. Ball smiled, feeling like the weight of the world had just been lifted off of his shoulder. Ball walked to Seven and embraced him.

"You're my nigga. I couldn't go through with it," Ball said as he released Seven.

"It wasn't a doubt in my mind, fam. After what we been through I knew there was no way. You all I got Ball . . . I mean Braylon." Seven said. They both began to laugh at Seven's little jab of sarcasm. Seven walked over to his mini bar and poured them both a glass of cognac. Seven was genuinely happy to have his partner in crime back. They sat back in the office and talked and agreed to let the past be the past. After thirty minutes, Seven decided it was time to let his crew know that Ball was not an enemy.

"Now the problem is to get these niggas to accept you," Seven said as he pointed at the goons having fun on the main floor. Ball looked through the window and saw everyone partying and having a goodtime.

"That might not be so easy," Ball said just before he took a deep breath. He knew that the label of being a snitch would forever be on him, but if Seven forgave him then he figured the crew would eventually do so.

"Okay, let me tell these niggas what it is. You come out after I introduce you, cool?" Seven said and downed the glass of cognac. He stood up and headed to the door. "I'm going to call you out . . . in style." Seven said as he grabbed the bottle on the table and headed out. Ball raised his glass and smiled. He understood at that moment that niggas like Seven came once in a lifetime. Seven was in a league of his own and Ball was honored to call him a friend. That type of loyalty will make a grown man cry. Ball watched through the double sided mirror and nervousness sat in as he wondered how they would take the news. He watched closely. Seven signaled for the band to stop playing for a moment as he walked onto the stage.

"Everybody! I need your attention. I'm about to make an announcement." Seven said as he spoke loudly so everyone could hear him. He looked over at his son who was standing on top of the bar which he was dancing on. "Come over here little man." Seven said to Rah. One of the goons helped him off the bar and Rah ran over to Seven. But one of the bunnies stopped Rah and she bent down and whispered in his ear. "Hold on sweetheart. You can't go up there right now," she said. "Now close your eyes."

Seven was so busy looking for Rah to come to him, he didn't see one of the bunnies walk up on him with a gun drawn. Instantly all of the bunnies dropped their trays and pulled out pistols that were tucked under their skirt or in their bra. Seven never saw it coming. Millie was the bunny in disguise. She was there to settle an old beef. All of the bunnies in the room worked for Millie and they all weren't afraid to put their murder game down. Seven's crew was defenseless and they all had just got caught slipping. It all seemed to happen in slow motion and Ball couldn't do anything but watch as she walked up on Seven and fired a hollow tip bullet clean through his head, killing him instantly. Ball's heart dropped as he saw Seven's limp body collapse to the floor. They had been ambushed and it happened right under their noses. Rah cried and rushed over to his father. He didn't understand what was going on. The only thing he wanted was for his father to wake up, but that would never happen.

"Noooooo!" Ball screamed as he looked on through the mirror. The whole crew was relieved of their guns, leaving them defenseless. Millie then stepped over Seven's body and spit on it. "I told you I would be back," she said as she wiped her lips and rushed out of the door. The sounds of grown men crying filled the room and they couldn't do anything about it.

With guns to their neck, the only thing they could do was watch. Once Millie got out of the door, the ladies followed as they all jumped into a van and peeled off. Ball dropped to his knees and tears came down. He knew that Seven's death was a direct result of him not killing Millie months before. Seven always told him to "finish his breakfast." He didn't do that and Seven's life was lost because of it. What Ball did was underestimate the power of a woman. Millie was cut from the same cloth as Seven, and Seven understood that. That's the reason he sent Ball to murk her because he knew it was only a matter of time before she got him. Ball quickly gathered himself and snuck out the back door . . . he knew he wasn't welcome in that room and it sent a dagger through his heart. He couldn't even go to the aide of Seven.

Ball eventually would get put in federal custody and never see Ohio again. His heart was ripped from him, knowing that he was the reason Seven was gone. Now he was alone. No Zoey, no Lola, and no Seven. He had no love. He couldn't go back to the streets because he would forever wear the name . . . Snitch.

A tear cascaded down the cheek of Ball's face as he opened his eyes. He had spilled his heart out to the reporter giving him every detail of his experience as a snitch. It was something that he had to get off of his chest, and he finally did so. He didn't want it to end the way it did, but Ball was hopeful that the young reporter would shed light on the real story.

"I still have nightmares of that moment. It plays in my head over and over again." Ball said as he wiped away his tear. "That man taught me so much in such a little time."

Chris Nicks wrote in his pad and walked circles around the table. He listened closely to Ball's story and soaked up every word. Over the six hours he took notes and recorded every word, wanting to get Ball's side of the candid story. Chris took a seat and took a deep breath, trying to take in all that he had heard. He put down his pad and reached into his bag and pulled out a medium sized envelope. He handed it to Ball.

"This is for you." Nicks said softly. Ball looked confused as he grabbed the envelope. He opened it and pulled out the pictures that were inside of it. He looked at the pictures and saw a beautiful woman on them pushing a little boy on a swing set. As Ball examined the pictures closely, the face became more familiar. It was Lola. She had gained a little weight and cut her hair short, but she was still as pretty as the day was long. Ball couldn't believe his eyes. It had been years since he had seen Lola. The last time he saw her, she was running into the woods in Aspen.

"You notice something," Nicks said as Ball's eyes stayed glued to the pictures.

"This is Lola," Ball whispered as he flipped through the pictures smiling.

"Look closer. That little boy resembles you, doesn't he?" Nicks said. Ball immediately paid attention to the young boy who looked to be about nine or ten years old. "That's your son. It seems like Lola wasn't alone when you last saw her in Aspen. She had a package with her." Nicks said.

"Are you saying . . ." Ball said as he looked at Nicks. Ball's heart skipped a beat when he saw the small caliber handgun pointed directly at him. "What the fuck?" he asked as he was startled.

"They live in Oklahoma under the witness protection program. And yeah, that's your son. But guess who's son I am?" Nicks said as he smiled and took off the non-prescription glasses. "Daddy always said I would be something special one day. I never thought I would be a writer. Funny how shit works out isn't it?" Nicks said. Nick had the small gun hidden in his boot and it worked like a charm. He got into journalism under a pen-name and he never would have thought that he would have the opportunity to avenge his father's death. But when the doors of opportunity arose, he walked through them gladly.

"Damn," Ball whispered as he took a deeper look into Nick's eyes and began to see who he really was. "You're Li'l Rah?" He said, realizing the truth. He kicked himself for not noticing something that was right under his nose for the past six hours.

"That's right. My father died right in front of me. He died right in front of me because of you," Rah said as he stood up while still pointing the gun at Ball.

"Look, I never meant it to happen like that. I didn't know Millie would come back and kill him." Ball pleaded as he put his hands in front of him. However, everything he said just fell on deaf ears. Unlike Ball, Rah was going to finish his breakfast . . . just like his father taught him. If Ball had finished his breakfast years ago, he wouldn't be in front of a barrel at this very moment.

"Say your peace with God," Rah said as he pressed the barrel to Ball's head. A moment of silence arose and Ball closed his eyes. He smiled thinking about how his son was a perfect blend of himself and Lola. Ball then murmured a few words and the sounds of two shots rung through the house leaving Ball laying face flat on the table, drowning in his own blood.

"Rest in peace, Daddy," Rah whispered as he looked down at the ground, knowing his father was *looking up* at him smiling.

Epilogue

Lola stood in front of the sink washing dishes as she stared outside and into her backyard. She looked over at the stove to check on the grilled cheese sandwich she was making for her son. She was expecting him any moment now. He should have been walking from the bus stop and on his way home. Lola wanted to make sure that her son was fed and taken care of because she planned on finally opening up the magazine that had been sitting on her coffee table for weeks. She couldn't bring herself to open it ever since she picked it up from the local news stand. That day particularly was a memorable date for her. It was the day that Seven was murdered. It had been exactly ten years ago to the day, and it hurt her heart that things ended the way they did. She picked up the magazine and looked at the cover and smiled. Seven graced the cover looking like a million bucks in his expensive Armani suit and diamond cufflinks. She then looked at the headline that read *Inside: the memoirs of a snitch*. She knew that she got off easy because her involvement wasn't documented like Ball's was. She had guilt that weighed heavily on her shoulders.

She knew that she had committed the ultimate deception by being a snitch but her hand was forced. She grew up hating drug dealers. While a typical ghetto child would have embraced the drug game after having a father like Bunkie Green, Lola hated it. Once she lost her mother to the drug and then her father, she developed hatred in her growing years and promised that she would make a difference in her community. As a child she loved and adored Bunkie Green. However, as she grew up in foster homes and orphanages she developed a deep hatred for him, and men like him. In her mind, Bunkie killed her mother rather than Teri's own addiction.

When she went off to college, she didn't tell anyone that the college she went to was a police academy. She was determined to help save someone's family and prevent a little girl's life being ruined by the trickle-down effect of drugs. She had suffered from both sides of the heroin game. She lost her mom to the addiction of the drug, and then her father to the greed it created in men.

When she became a federal agent, she vowed to take down any and every man that resembled her father and Seven fit that mold to the tee. What she didn't anticipate is the strong relationship and comradeship that she gained from running with Seven and the Goon Squad. She dedicated three years of her life to living a lie and it took a toll on her mentally.

Years back, when Ball let her escape she wasn't alone. She had Michael "Ball" Green in her stomach. She knew that she had a chance to make a difference in someone's life directly when she found out she was pregnant. So, she quit the force and went into seclusion to raise her son. It was not a day that went by that she didn't think of Seven. She always would think about what happened to Rah and she always wanted to go back and save him, but how could she raise the son of a man that she was deceiving for so many years? These were the type of questions that she asked over the years that almost drove her crazy. She looked at the magazine and smiled as tears began to flow.

"Rest in peace, Seven. I will always love you, bro," she said as she wiped her tears away. She heard her son open the front door followed by the sound of his angelic and enthusiastic voice.

"Mom! I'm home!" Li'l Ball yelled as he made his way to the kitchen. Lola quickly wiped away her tears and put on a fake smile, not wanting her son to see her like that.

"Hey, baby boy!" she said as he walked in and hugged her. Lola hugged him tightly and remembered what her purpose of living was. Li'l Ball was her pride and joy, and he gave her a new take on life. She was honored to have an opportunity to raise a child and shield him from the things she had to see at a young age. Ball's age was significant for Lola as she felt like it was the age her life ended. However, she was proud to say Li'l Ball's life was just getting underway. She smiled and hugged him tightly. She let him go and he stepped back and smiled.

"I love you mom. You give the best hugs," he said as he gave her his charming smile. His dimples were so deep, she could put nickels in them and there was no better sight in the world in Lola's eyes. She thought about Ball and how much her son resembled his father. She always wished that he was able to see his son, but she knew that she would be playing with fire if she tried to locate him. So she decided to keep that chapter in her life closed.

"I love you too," she said as he made a tear drop from her eyes.

"Why are you crying?' he asked.

"Because I'm happy baby boy," she simply said. "Because I'm happy."

A knock at the door, interrupted their special moment and Lola instantly looked toward the front door. She wiped away her tears once again and opened her door. It was a young man with nerdy glasses and a small frame standing before her.

"Hi, may I help you?" Lola asked as she looked at the young man.

"Hello Ma'am. My name is Chris Nicks and I'm from Fed magazine. I was wondering if I could have a little bit of your time."

THE END

Notes

Notes

Notes

ORDER FORM
URBAN BOOKS, LLC
78 E. Industry Ct
Deer Park, NY 11729

Name: (please print):_____

Address: _____

City/State: _____

Zip: _____

QTY	TITLES	PRICE
	16 On The Block	$14.95
	A Girl From Flint	$14.95
	A Pimp's Life	$14.95
	Baltimore Chronicles	$14.95
	Baltimore Chronicles 2	$14.95
	Betrayal	$14.95
	Black Diamond	$14.95
	Black Diamond 2	$14.95
	Black Friday	$14.95
	Both Sides Of The Fence	$14.95
	Both Sides Of The Fence 2	$14.95
	California Connection	$14.95

Shipping and handling-add $3.50 for 1st book, then $1.75 for each additional book.
Please send a check payable to:
Urban Books, LLC
Please allow 4-6 weeks for delivery

ORDER FORM
URBAN BOOKS, LLC
78 E. Industry Ct
Deer Park, NY 11729

Name: (please print):_____

Address: _____

City/State: _____

Zip: _____

QTY	TITLES	PRICE
	California Connection 2	$14.95
	Cheesecake And Teardrops	$14.95
	Congratulations	$14.95
	Crazy In Love	$14.95
	Cyber Case	$14.95
	Denim Diaries	$14.95
	Diary Of A Mad First Lady	$14.95
	Diary Of A Stalker	$14.95
	Diary Of A Street Diva	$14.95
	Diary Of A Young Girl	$14.95
	Dirty Money	$14.95
	Dirty To The Grave	$14.95

Shipping and handling-add $3.50 for 1st book, then $1.75 for each additional book.
Please send a check payable to:
  Urban Books, LLC
Please allow 4-6 weeks for delivery

ORDER FORM
URBAN BOOKS, LLC
78 E. Industry Ct
Deer Park, NY 11729

Name: (please print): _____

Address: _____

City/State: _____

Zip: _____

QTY	TITLES	PRICE
	Gunz And Roses	$14.95
	Happily Ever Now	$14.95
	Hell Has No Fury	$14.95
	Hush	$14.95
	If It Isn't love	$14.95
	Kiss Kiss Bang Bang	$14.95
	Last Breath	$14.95
	Little Black Girl Lost	$14.95
	Little Black Girl Lost 2	$14.95
	Little Black Girl Lost 3	$14.95
	Little Black Girl Lost 4	$14.95
	Little Black Girl Lost 5	$14.95

Shipping and handling-add $3.50 for 1st book, then $1.75 for each additional book.
Please send a check payable to:
Urban Books, LLC
Please allow 4-6 weeks for delivery

ORDER FORM
URBAN BOOKS, LLC
78 E. Industry Ct
Deer Park, NY 11729

Name: (please print): _____

Address: _____

City/State: _____

Zip: _____

QTY	TITLES	PRICE
	Loving Dasia	$14.95
	Material Girl	$14.95
	Moth To A Flame	$14.95
	Mr. High Maintenance	$14.95
	My Little Secret	$14.95
	Naughty	$14.95
	Naughty 2	$14.95
	Naughty 3	$14.95
	Queen Bee	$14.95
	Say It Ain't So	$14.95
	Snapped	$14.95
	Snow White	$14.95

Shipping and handling-add $3.50 for 1st book, then $1.75 for each additional book.
Please send a check payable to:
Urban Books, LLC
Please allow 4-6 weeks for delivery

ORDER FORM
URBAN BOOKS, LLC
78 E. Industry Ct
Deer Park, NY 11729

Name: (please print): _____

Address: _____

City/State: _____

Zip: _____

QTY	TITLES	PRICE
	Spoil Rotten	$14.95
	Supreme Clientele	$14.95
	The Cartel	$14.95
	The Cartel 2	$14.95
	The Cartel 3	$14.95
	The Dopefiend	$14.95
	The Dopeman Wife	$14.95
	The Prada Plan	$14.95
	The Prada Plan 2	$14.95
	Where There Is Smoke	$14.95
	Where There Is Smoke 2	$14.95

Shipping and handling-add $3.50 for 1st book, then $1.75 for each additional book.

Please send a check payable to:
Urban Books, LLC
Please allow 4-6 weeks for delivery